Hopelessly SHATTERED

BINK CUMMINGS

Proofreader/Editor- Kristina Canady & Genevieve Scholl

Proofreader/Beta- Mary Bevinger, Tammy Anderson & Barbara Clark Green.

Cover Designer- Bink Cummings

Photo provided from: Big Stock

Dedication

For all of the strong, independent, single mothers out
there
who are looking for a second chance at love...
or to enact a sense of revenge on an ex you loathe.

Bink Cummings

Recognition

I wanted to say a quick, and much deserved thanks to Mary for being my #1 cheerleader throughout this books entire process. She helped me immensely—reading chapter after chapter as I wrote, and doing last minute proofreading just to find the stragglers. I can't thank her enough from the bottom of my heart. I love ya, chick!

Thank you Kylie and Tammy for listening to me nonstop, and helping read this book as it came along, giving me feedback where it was needed. You two are fantastic! I love ya both, bunches and bunches!

<u>Note</u>

For those who have read MC Chronicles: The Diary of Bink Cummings, this book takes place in the span of time between Vol 1 and Vol 2.

Bink Cummings

Driving down a dark road in the middle of Bumfuck Egypt, six months pregnant and starving, wasn't exactly how I pictured my relaxing Thanksgiving vacation going. I wanted to stay home with my two daughters, celebrate the holiday with stuffing and the carved bird that my mother, Shelly, always cooks to perfection. The thought of missing her green bean casserole and those buttered biscuits, is seriously making me rethink my plan to come down to Texas. Yet, here I am, on my way to meet a man I've only spoken to ten, or so times in the past month. No, it's not some secret sexy rendezvous. I'm hopefully going to get some answers about my past that might fill in some blanks. I'd tried to do it over the phone or *Skype.* However, Bear... *yes, that's actually his name* ... refused to disclose anything unless it's face to face. Generally, I'd consider that creepy, and probably a bit ax-murderish. But, beggars can't be choosers. And after fourteen years of unanswered questions, I'm willing to take what I can get. Anything is better than nothing. Which is precisely what I know—squat.

As I travel down this never-ending highway of clouded blackness, grass, and trees, how about I fill you in on the finer details of myself, and my foolish plan to waste a perfectly good vacation with a man named Bear? Does that sound good? Well, I sure hope so because I'm bored out of my damn mind. The radio in this old Malibu doesn't work, and the AC when it's running, sounds like a chicken dying. If they'd had anything else I could afford at the rental lot, I would have gotten it. Having two daughters and another one on the way, I'm not exactly rolling in the dough. Not when I work as a librarian, and I'm saving up money for my daughters'—everything. They're girls—notoriously expensive. Having one who's nine years old and the other at eight, I know firsthand what the future holds. Just think about it: three periods, a lifetime supply of *Midol* and chocolate, three prom dresses, three girls with shoe addictions, three different bra and panty sizes. God forbid they're stacked like me. Then I'll be really fucked, having to buy fifty dollar bras that are ugly as hell and only used for function. Sheesh, I'm getting a damn headache just thinking about it...

Anywho...

Sorry about the tangent. I seem to get a little sidetracked and overwhelmed when dollar signs keep adding up. If you have daughters, I'm sure you can relate... Let's get back to what I was saying about this trip. I guess I should give you the basics first. My dad died when I was fourteen in an explosive car accident, just like the ones seen in the movies. There wasn't a body to bury. His headstone is merely that— a piece of marble with his name etched in remembrance. It's resting between my grandpa and great-grandparents in a cemetery right outside of town. Sure, it serves as a place for my grandma to visit and mourn the tragic loss of her son. On the flipside, it's a nagging reminder of the lack of evidence surrounding his death. His DNA was recovered at the scene, as was part of his driver's license, and the car that was obviously his. It was the same *Camaro* he'd left in that night. It was his party car. Brand new. Sleek lines. The envy of all my friends in school, because I had the cool dad who drove a fast car and spoiled me rotten. I'm not sure what they expected when I'm an only child.

When I was six, my parents divorced and shared 50/50 custody of me. Except my mother, who wanted the divorce in the first place, didn't really want to uphold her share. She was more focused on the child support my dad dutifully paid her than caring about me. By the time I turned eight, she up and left. Moved clear across the country to Las Vegas, leaving me to be raised by my dad and grandma. Not that I minded. She wasn't a good mother anyhow. Sure, I visited her twice a year, two weeks in the summer and a week at either Christmas or Thanksgiving, but the rest of the year we never spoke. She soon became a stranger to me, and the bond my daddy and I shared grew stronger by the day. He became my sole provider. My best friend. The man I looked up to. My hero.

For years, we'd take our weekly drives along the countryside just to talk about anything and everything. And if we weren't talking, we were singing to old school rock music as he tapped his fingers on the steering wheel or drank a can of beer. He always had the greatest cassette tape collection, which we'd rewind over and over again to our favorites. They varied all the way from *Guns N' Roses* to *AC/DC* to *Ozzy*. There was never a dull moment in my life. I learned to cook, thanks to my grandma, since my dad was terrible at it. He taught me how to do the laundry, to shoot pool in our basement game room, and how to perform basic maintenance on cars. We went on daddy-daughter dates weekly to a nearby steakhouse so we could gorge on some juicy porterhouses, and he could get his fill of draught beer. We even took short, out of town hotel vacations once a month. It was the life, and I wouldn't have changed it for the world...

Then, one spring morning, everything flipped upside down. To this day, I can vividly replay that memory like it happened just yesterday...

Beep, Beep, Beep, *the alarm clock sounded. Prying my eyes open and rubbing the sleep from them, I turned my head and glared at the noisy abomination that sat on the floor next to my floor length mirror—7:05 AM. It was time to get up and get ready for school. Last night, Daddy had left me home by myself so he could party with his friends. He'd set the number he could be reached at on the table next to the phone. Which meant I had exactly twenty minutes to get dressed before I woke him up from a hangover, so he could drive me to school. It'd take me at least ten minutes to rouse him enough to throw on his shoes and shuffle out of the house with his morning can of* Dew *in hand. I hate mornings like this. Then again, I guess it beat the alternative of him partying at home when I had year-end exams.*

Sliding off my bed, the sunlight cut through the shades, casting lines across my pink carpet. The doorbell rang, and I peeked at my clock one more time—7:07 AM. Who in the heck could be at our house this early in the morning?

Knowing that my dad wasn't going to wake up by the mere ringing of the doorbell, I tossed on a pair of pajama pants over my underwear and made haste through the living room as it sounded again. Pushing through the final door that separated our living room from our front sunroom, I stopped dead in my tracks when I saw an officer standing on the porch staring back at me through the window. Sliding back the deadbolt, I opened the door wide, wondering if I should've woken Dad up first.

"Hello, Officer. Can I help you?" My voice was groggy with sleep, and a little shaky as I stood in the doorframe.

"Are you related to Michael Remington?" he asked.

Ummm ... okay.

I nodded. "Yes. That's my dad. Why?"

"Miss, is anyone else home with you?" he inquired, glancing around me to see if anyone else was on my tail. Unless he had a jackhammer, my dad wouldn't be walking out here anytime soon. He's worse to wake up than I am. It was a chore that I hated. But if I didn't do it, I'd have to walk the five miles to school. At fourteen, I was not going to do that.

I tucked my arms over my chest. "Just my dad."

Keeping firm eye contact, the officer shifted uncomfortably on his feet. "Does a relative live nearby?"

I shook my head. "No. Sorry."

Sighing long and hard, he set his shoulders back. "Miss, I regret to inform you that Michael Remington was killed in a car crash at 2:30 this morning on route six."

Whoosh went the air in my lungs as tears pricked my eyes.

I took a staggered step backward.

This has to be a joke, right? A sick and twisted one.

I almost laughed at the lunacy.

"What?!" I shrieked instead.

"Miss, why don't you go inside and sit down? I'll wait until an adult arrives to be with you. You shouldn't be alone." He started walking forward, automatically making me take a step back, then another and another until my shocked frame fell into a lump on our couch. The urge to run into the bedroom and shake my dad awake clawed at my insides.

Dead? He can't be dead! He's supposed to take me to school today. I have tests. I ... I ... This can't be happening!

A phone was thrust into my hand. I stared at it blankly. What am I supposed to do with this?

"You need to call someone, Miss," the officer explained.

Oh ... right ... I have to... Oh. My. God. My Dad really is dead?! I really have to call my grandma and tell her, and my uncle, and my mom. I haven't even spoken to my mom in ages. I don't want to call her. I don't want to call anyone. I want to go back to bed and forget this day ever happened! This has to be a dream! He has to be sleeping.

Tossing the phone onto the couch, I moved to stand. In a flash, the officer's in front of me, blocking the way. "Miss, where are you going?"

Tilting my head back to look him in the eye, my body froze in place, and everything went numb. "I have to go wake my dad up. This has to be a mistake." My hand that I could no longer feel somehow pointed toward the hallway.

A pitiful expression morphed his features as he rubbed the corner of his eye with his knuckle. Gently, he then grabbed hold of my shoulders. "Sweetie, your dad isn't in there. He was in a car accident this morning. He and one of his friends hit a tree and died. I'm so sorry." Emotions clogged his throat as he spoke.

He's dead!

Oh. My. God.

This is real!

With his gentle guidance, I sat back down and made the first of many horrific phone calls to my family. How do you tell your grandmother that her son was killed? How do you make it easier on them? Do you tell them to sit down? Do you break it easy? Or do you rip it off like a band-aid? I didn't know what to do. So I did the only thing I could. I picked up the old, clunky cordless phone and dialed her number.

She picked up on the second ring. "Hello?"

I clutched the phone firmly, pain radiating through my white-knuckled grasp. "Grandma, it's me, Kat. Are you sitting down?"

Over the course of the next hour, I made five phone calls, all of which robbed me of my childhood one chunk at a time. Nobody believed me when I told them that Dad was dead. Plus, each and every one of them demanded to speak to the police officer to make sure what I said was true. Every conversation ended with the same, "Hang in there, we'll be there soon." And they were. All day long, my childhood home overflowed with family and friends. Some of which I hadn't seen in years. They offered their sincere condolences and gave me big hugs. The officer stayed by my side for hours, talking to the family and making sure I was okay. I could tell he felt sorry for me. Everyone did. Abandoned by my mother at eight, only to lose my dad at fourteen.

Over the next few days, bits and pieces of his death were disclosed. Like how his car exploded when it impacted the tree, because his NOS reserve turned the car into a bomb. How the man who was in the passenger seat with him was incinerated along with my Dad. That the only DNA found was small bits of charred bone fragments and very little blood. The explosion basically ruined any chance of either family getting true closure.

A week later, we had a funeral, which was nothing more than an empty box sent to rest in the ground. Our family had filled it with mementos of our time with him. I honestly don't remember a whole lot, other than that. I'd went into shock, refusing to cry, as I puked my guts out constantly. It all got worse after my mother showed up to his funeral, claiming she was taking me back to Las Vegas with her a week later. Which was precisely what happened, since she still had 50/50 custody per their agreement.

In a matter of two weeks, my dad died, we buried a box, I packed up my belongings, and was forced to leave my childhood home, family, friends, and, most importantly, my grandma. It was horrible. All of it. The cutthroat fights to try and get me to stay, which I wanted to. The emotional plane ride to Las Vegas. My mom's sad attempt to play mother of the year. The little two-bedroom apartment she shared with her unemployed, junkie boyfriend. It was a horrifying nightmare come to life in vivid, breathing color.

Eventually, after the dust had settled and I started school in Vegas, I couldn't stop thinking about all of those unanswered questions about the guy in my dad's car, and the party he'd been at. I was no fool, even at fourteen. I knew my father was involved in some shady business, and that he hung out with a rougher crowd. None of that could've changed my views on him, though. To me, he was still my hero, regardless of whatever business he was involved in.

At sixteen, I went back home to Indiana to visit my grandma over the summer. One day, I overheard my uncle saying that he was worried my dad might have been murdered because he was a drug dealer. My dad and drugs was never on the radar. I never saw him sell anything, and he surely wasn't a junkie. I'd seen plenty of them. Sure, he smoked cigarettes and drank beer. Albeit, he sometimes drank and drove, even with me in the passenger seat. That was how I was raised and hadn't thought twice about it.

Then, when I got older, my mother told me things—like how she divorced him because he'd been growing marijuana in a friend's garage, and that he'd went on secret trips to distribute the pot they grew. Really, I'm not sure if my mother should have told me that stuff. It helped create a monster in my head. I wanted to know more. I needed to know if my dad was murdered, or if I'm really making something out of nothing.

On my eighteenth birthday, I inherited my father's life insurance money and left Vegas to move back home where my grandma needed me. Where I needed to be to finally get some answers. Answers that my mother refused to let me investigate or help me with. Sure, we'd grown somewhat closer over the four years I'd lived with her. She sort of became a friend, but definitely not a mother. Shelly could never be that to me, no matter how hard she's tried. My grandma has and always will be the mother I never truly had. There's no changing that. What can I say?

I'm a firm believer that if you want to be treated like a mother, then you should act like one. Unfortunately, my mom doesn't actually possess that ability.

So, yeah, I got home and did my research. Lots of it. Found some interesting things that didn't add up. The reports of his death were now missing from the courthouse. It was interesting that guys he used to hang with, some of which were at that party that night, wouldn't agree to speak to me either. Not even when I desperately showed up at their houses, called them, or drove to their place of employment, would they give me the time of day. The more I checked into things, the less I found. Yet, the more suspicious his death became. Nothing added up. The pieces of the puzzle never quite fit right.

Fast forward a year ... I was living in the cute, three bedroom bungalow I'd purchased with the insurance money when my life began to transform. While researching my father's death the best I could with limited resources, a sexy man moved in next door to me ... and I'm sure you can guess what happened next. I'm not going to go into great details, because the more I think about it, the more painful it becomes. That's a part of my life I choose to ignore. A stupid time that gave me two of the most precious gifts a woman could ever ask for—my daughters, Roxie and Scarlett.

His name was Brent, and he was every woman's wet dream. Trust me, I saw it everywhere we went. The way they ogled him. The way he smiled like he knew just how sexy he was. Then the women's eyes would shift to me with blatant disgust. Let's just say

I'm not the kind of woman you'd picture with a man like Brent. He was six foot three and built like a brick shit house. His muscles had muscles. Though, they weren't grossly oversized. They were what first had me asking him to help with this grill I'd stupidly bought, but couldn't seem to get out of the back of my *Suburban* without giving myself a hernia. His shirtless body hoisting that grill was a thing of beauty. His bald head and blue eyes didn't hurt the picture either. Needless to say, that was the day I swooned, and the rest was pretty much history.

Anyhow...

Enough about that. He flirted like he was God's gift to women, and I was the young and dumb, chunky nerd from next door, who ate that up in spades.

Okay. Let's get this straight: I'm not unfortunate looking. I'm just not the type of woman who dates muscle bound men who women drool over. I usually attract the average Joes since I'm the average girl-next-door. I'm five foot three on a good day. I wear glasses—those black rimmed ones that people imagine naughty teachers wearing. My hair is naturally light blonde, and it falls in loose waves down the middle of my back as it always has. I have bright teal eyes, a perky nose, tons of freckles, and a body with curves that just won't stop. I'd say I have an hourglass figure, but not a skinny one by any stretch of the imagination. Before my girls were born—we'll get into that in a minute—I was relatively happy with my body. After kids, as I'm sure you can imagine, I got bigger. Things never go back the same after stretch marks, and all that pregnancy jazz wreaks havoc over your poor body. It took me years to get back to some semblance of my normal. Now that I'm pregnant again, another challenge to fight off the baby weight will soon begin.

Hold up a second. Pause the story. I think this is my turn. Easing on my brake, the green street sign to my right reflects in the car's headlights—Durnst Avenue. Yes. That's it. Turning, I'm met with another long road of the same shit—as predicted. More grass. More trees. Where's the damn city? Peeking down at my cell phone, that keeps losing signal, it says I'm fifteen miles from my destination. I exhale a relieved breath. Well, it's about damn time.

As I was saying, Brent and I dated. If that's what you'd call hanging out all the time and becoming best friends. Three months into this *friendship,* we had sex. Then we kept having sex. And as the story goes, I became pregnant. During my pregnancy, we fell in love. Or I fell in love with him. Apparently, he never felt the same. Roxie was born, and as soon as I was able to have sex again, we did—like bunnies. Which resulted in another pregnancy. That's why my daughters are only eleven months apart, to the day...

Fast forward three months after little Scarlett was born ... and you've got me waking up next to a stack of hundred dollar bills on the bedside table, and a note. *A fucking note!*

Kat,

I'm sorry. I can't do this anymore. It's been fun. Take care of the girls. I'll send you more money when I can. I know you'll raise them right.

Sincerely, Me

Yep. A real coward's way out. Sayonara, Brent. Sayonara, my dreams. *Poof!* He'd vanished into thin air. His house next door was vacant like he'd never been there. There wasn't a trace of him to be seen, aside from a few measly pictures I'd secretly snuck whenever he wasn't looking. I was alone once more with two infants, a library job, and no family. Aside from my aging grandma, who had a hard enough time taking care of herself. If it weren't for my mother taking pity on my crazy circumstances, I would have raised those little turds all by myself. Thankfully, after a sobbing phone call to my mom the day after Brent disappeared, she left her junkie boyfriend in Vegas and moved back home to help me out. A place she said she'd never return to. Yet did, for me.

A month after she came to help me put my life back together, she'd bought a small, two bedroom house a block from mine. The perfect distance to give us our own privacy, and once the girls got old enough, easy enough for them to ride their bikes over to anytime they want. Which is a lot. They adore their grandma Shelly. She spoils them rotten.

I guess that's basically my life in a nutshell, aside from the past six months. Which includes another unplanned pregnancy—that I don't want to discuss right now—and Bear hitting me up on *Facebook* after he saw my old post on a website asking for any information about my dad.

It was a Sunday afternoon four weeks ago when the friend request popped up. *Bear Prez* was the man's name, and his profile picture was nothing more than a patch that said Sacred Sinners on the top rocker and Texas on the bottom. In the middle was a stitched design that had three skulls in front of a five pointed star, that also had roses surrounding it and some wings. It was pretty badass and scary in equal measure. The strange thing was: I'd seen that patch a hundred times before. We have a local MC by the same name, using the same patch, only a few towns over. So when I messaged him to see how we knew each other before accepting or rejecting him, all he replied was...

Got some information about Mike. Saw your post and wanted to swap stories.

My heart stopped, and I responded immediately.

You knew my dad?!

Yes. You're his only daughter. He was married to Shelly until you were six. Then they got divorced.

All of that was a matter of public record so I wasn't convinced.

Okay. Tell me more, so I know you're not just some creep.

Two days went by as I waited with bated breath for another reply. Stalking my *Facebook* messages between motherhood duties and working became a new hobby.

Finally, as I was fixing the girls chicken soup for dinner, a short response came...

Listen, I can't talk on here. It's not secure. My name's Jake Knox, aka Bear. You can check it out if you want. I'm the president of the Sacred Sinners MC chapter here in Texas.

Attached to his simple message was a picture of him wearing a vest. On the breast was the name Bear and president, verifying what he said was true. His face was aged, but not terribly so. He had buzzed gray hair on top of his head and a long, dark gray beard that was braided down his front. His forearms that were tucked across his barrel chest were littered with tattoos. And his eyes I couldn't make out because they were shielded behind a pair of cool sunglasses. One look at this man and I knew two things for certain. One: that his name suited him perfectly. He was as big as a bear. And two: I knew I could trust his word. I couldn't tell you why I felt that way and still do to this day. It just sunk in. He was too honest and forward to pose any real threat to me.

My dad taught me from an early age to trust my gut. So that's what I did. I trusted my gut. And now here I am, visiting Bear in Texas over Thanksgiving break, hoping to gather any sort of info about my dad's death. It beats dwelling on the fact that another envelope of cash was delivered to my house forty-eight hours ago. They come every few months. A couple thousand dollars made up of hundred dollar bills. No note. No card. Nothing. Then again, I already know who it's from—Brent. It's his sad contribution to our daughters' lives. I guess it's better than nothing.

That's enough about him...

Turning the final curve, the lights to the left draw my attention just as my phone's GPS declares I'm yards from my destination. Pressing on the brake, I ease forward, my gaze glued on the zoo of bikes lining the entire front and side yard of the house. If that's what you'd call it. Not sure that I would. It appears to be an old boarding school or something. The place is set back just a ways from this desolate road. No cars are coming or going. No street lights. No signs. Just a short driveway, a massive white building with oversized windows that cast light from the indoors along the grass, and classic rock music pulsing through the muggy night air.

Taking a deep breath, I turn into the gravel drive, just now noticing the men and women frolicking like drunken children in the opposing side yard. Guess this is the place. Although, I'm not exactly sure what I was expecting. I know Bear is an MC prez, and I figured he'd want to meet where there'd be witnesses. What I didn't expect was this. How big is his club, anyhow? I mean, I know the one locally isn't tiny. But this looks much larger than that. There have to be at least fifty bikes here in all shapes and sizes. Not that I know much about motorcycles. I've never even been on one. My dad said they were too dangerous for me. And Brent—well, let's just say he wasn't fond of me liking anything cool like that. Anytime I'd comment about one when it would pass by, he'd cringe. Don't worry. I got the memo loud and clear—no motorcycles for Kat. Which is fine. I'm more of a truck gal, anyhow.

Parking my car midway up the drive, next to a row of chrome, I scan my surroundings like my dad always taught, before unlocking the doors and climbing out with my cell phone in hand. You can never be too careful.

A woman and man tumble naked on the grass a few feet away as I walk across the gravel to the wide porch, trying not to gape at the display.

"Can I help ya?" a massive bald man wearing a leather vest asks, blocking my way to the door. For a moment, my mind wanders, as it always does when I see bald men. For a second, their noses sharpen to match Brent's as their eyes lighten to mimic his blue. That dimple at the crease of his lip always manifests in the precise spot, messing with my head. Then, I blink twice, and all is right in the world. The shards from my shattered heart are brushed away, and the dread quickly retreats, returning me back to my kind of normal. Whatever that is.

I exhale in relief.

"Ma'am, can I help ya?" he asks again, this time tilting his head to the side, regarding me from head to toe like I'm some adorable puppy he wants to pet. Casually, as if it's second nature, he tucks his arms across his big chest, showing off a colorful array of inked flesh.

Drawing my shoulders back, one hand on my hip and the other cupping my growing belly, I reply, "Yes. I came here to see Bear."

A smirk quirks from the corner of his lips that looks almost evil in the dim glow that caresses the covered porch. "No offense, princess, you're not his type." A small chuckle proceeds, and I leer, unamused.

"I'm not here to suck his dick. I'm here to talk."

Wow. I'm sassy tonight. Decorum isn't my strong suit.

Baldy rears his head back as if my words have shocked him. I get that a lot. You don't picture a woman like me to smart off as I do. Too bad. Ya get what ya get.

"You're feisty," he remarks.

"And you're observant. Now, can I please see Bear?"

See, not all my manners have disappeared, I said *please*.

Glancing over his shoulder at the door then back to me, he pensively rubs the top of his head. "You're not exactly party material, doll." His eyes dip to my belly.

Son of a bitch. I don't have time for this shit. I haven't eaten in hours, and my blood sugar has to be getting low. Already having two kids, I learned quickly that me and starving are not a good thing. On top of that, I didn't travel all fucking day to be held up by some attractive goon in a vest that says Marco Polo on it. What kind of name is that, anyway?

Losing patience, my last strand of sanity snaps like a guitar string. "Listen, I'm here to talk to Bear. I don't care what y'all get down with here. You could be fucking pink-wigged clowns with whoopee cushion asses for all I give a hoot. I just know that I traveled all day to get here, and some hot guy isn't gonna stop me from getting inside to find out what I came here for. So, you need to tell me what I gotta do to see Bear, or so help me..." Let's just pray Mr. Marco Polo heeds my irritability, because nobody wants to fight a pregnant chick.

Holding his hands up in mock surrender, Marco Polo's toothy grin gets ten sizes too big for taking me seriously. Great, he still thinks I'm being cute. It's gotta be my height, ponytail, and these damn glasses. I look like a fucking librarian. Oh, right. I am one. It doesn't help that I am in leggings, black ballet flats, and my flowy white top that doesn't exactly scream biker babe. I get it. If he could see my mom bra or maternity panties, I'm sure he'd be in stitches. *Fucking men.*

"Listen, doll, there's fuckin' goin' on in there, and I don't want you to get yourself hurt. But ... if you really wanna see Bear, I'll let ya pass. Though, I gotta search ya first, to make sure you're not carrying—"

"What?" I interject, grabbing my belly and rubbing it with both hands. "You worried about this baby bomb I've got hidden under my shirt? Or how about the gun I've got shoved up my pussy? Or maybe the ounce of coke hidden inside my fat ass? What else do you wanna know? Where the detonation device is? It's my clit, asshole. So why don't you get on your knees to test it out yourself with your tongue? Or is that too personal?"

Eyes bulging, Mr. Marco's jaw all but hits the ground at the same moment I realize every ounce of bullshit I just spewed aloud. Mortified like never before, my cheeks catch fire. I cannot believe I let him uncage the crazy chick. I've usually got a better hold on her than this. Damn it! I try so hard to reign in my emotions. But when they rise, sometimes I say shit that I wouldn't normally.

Pressing my lips together, patiently waiting for his shock to wear off, I throttle the urge to beg for entrance. Why didn't I just let him frisk me? Where's the harm in that? I'm not a china doll. I'm not gonna break.

Shaking his head, mouth finally coming to a close, Mr. Baldy clears his throat. "I'm—"

The door behind him opens, severing his words as both of us glance at the attractive, pregnant woman filling the frame—well, partially filling it. She's skinny as hell, aside from the obvious bump that's close to the size of mine. I'm willing to bet she's a few months further along than me. I've always shown early. First kid, I was in maternity clothes from four months on. Second, from three months. This one, almost immediately. I blame it on my short stature. Then again, what the hell do I know?

"Marco, are you giving this woman crap?" The smile she offers is one of genuine mirth.

Marco rubs his head again, eyeing her then me before his chin lifts in my direction. "She wants to see Bear."

"So?" The woman absentmindedly rubs her belly, which is framed by a vest similar to Marco Polo's. On the chest, the name Vanessa is stitched on a pink patch.

"I have to search her," he mumbles uncertainly under his breath.

Vanessa's brows pinch as she scowls in his direction. "Seriously, Marco? She's pregnant, and attending a club party. Plus, you can tell by her accent she's not from 'round here. Let her pass before

I tell Ryker you were hassling our pregnant guest."
The woman doesn't wait for Marco's reply when she
reaches past him and grasps my forearm, pulling me
inside. She shuts the door in her wake, her long black
hair flinging in obvious defiance.

Releasing my arm, she nods toward the entrance.
"Sorry about him. He's new to our chapter. He's not
used to the small town way we run things. It's like
he's expecting people to mow down the place in a
drive by."

"That's not gonna happen, is it?" I ask stupidly. Of
course, it's not.

Smiling sweetly, she shakes her head, and pivots
on her heel, waddling further into the house. Not
knowing what to do, I trail after her, soaking in the
vastness. To the left, there's a wide room with tall
ceilings, a bar, pool tables, and a cluster of leather-
clad people hanging out. On the right is a living room,
complete with an oversized sectional sofa and big
screen TV. For a moment, I wish that's all I can see,
but it's not. Women and men in various displays of
lewdness are sprawled out on the couch and
hardwood floor, seemingly oblivious to being
watched, or not caring one iota that they are. I sort of
admire their openness. I've never been that secure in
myself to go topless, let alone permit a man to suck
my tits for all to see. Whatever trips their triggers, I
guess. I'm not one to judge.

Wading deeper into the bowels of the house, the
scent of mary-jane hangs in the air. They must have a
smoking room in here somewhere. I glance around,

observing a line of closed doors with no markings, and a set of stairs are straight ahead.

Stopping, Vanessa waits on me, and I take a long look at the back of her vest. It reads *Property of Ryker* on it. Guess that explains why she's here. Ryker must be her husband.

"He will probably be in his office."

She points down the hall to her right as I slide up beside her, just now noticing how much taller and skinnier she is than me. Vanessa has to be at least five foot ten and a hundred and twenty pounds soaking wet. If only we could all be that beautiful and statuesque. She looks like she should be on the cover of a maternity magazine. Even her jeans hug her perfect ass nicely. Not that I'm checking her ass out. I don't swing that way.

"Thanks for your help." I touch her arm to express my gratitude. "So what's he like?"

"Who?"

"Bea—"

My words stop short as a man yells, "Babe!" from behind us seconds before his arms affectionately wrap around Vanessa's growing belly.

She giggles like a girl in love, and I turn my head to see this man who's captured her heart. A tiny fraction of jealousy bubbles to the surface for an instant. Then as my eyes cast upon the man holding her, my entire world stops dead in its tracks. My brain short circuits. Air seizes in my lungs. A wound that I've tended for years tears open and swallows me whole as I take a staggering step to the side. My hands shake, eyes unblinking.

It can't be!

Oh my fucking god!

This can't be real!

It can't be him!

My eyes rake those muscles I've intimately touched. They look the same hidden under a layer of ink. The sharpness of his jaw is just as I remember, as is the fullness of his lips. Even the masculine curve of his ear is on point.

It ... It's him.

"Brent?!" I screech at the very moment his eyes sweep to the side, noticing my stricken expression.

Another staggering step backward and I meet the hall wall, slumping against it to keep my knees from buckling. The air whooshes from my lungs, and I suck in a pained breath only to hold it once more.

What the fuck?!

"Kat?" His disbelieving tone stabs my ear drums like hundreds of bee stings. I cover them and slide to the ground, knees drawn up for protection. Closing my eyes, I pray that this nightmare dissolves into a dream of colorful unicorns, and hot alpha men who don't abandon their families. This can't be my real life. I have to be sleeping. This can't be happening!

A firm hand touches my knee as I sense more bodies looming nearby.

Plugging my ears harder and squeezing my eyes tighter, I mumble a scratchy, "I just came here to find out about my dad. I just want to know what happened to my father. I don't need to see Brent. Didn't mean to see Brent." I start to rock. "Please leave me alone."

Grumbled masculine voices clash in the space that feels as if it's closing in on me. Another hand touches my knee. I jiggle my leg to knock it off, which does no good. It doesn't move. The air in my lungs surges in sharp pants. Lightheadedness forces my brain to churn. Sweat drips down the sides of my cheeks, dampening my palms. Every part of my frame vibrates in tiny tremors.

"Please go away," I beg like a child, uncaring if I sound pathetic.

That man ... I can't be around him. I just can't. They don't know what he did to me. To us. How he shattered me by disappearing. It took me over a year to feel normal again. To stop crying every night at the loss. Yet another man to abandon me. One by death and the other by choice. What the hell is with men in my life leaving?

I shake my head to clear it.

I don't have time for this distraction. My job only gave me three days off. Brent wasn't in my plans. I was to come here, find out about my dad, leave, then go to the hotel for the night. Nothing more. Nothing less. What the hell am I supposed to do now?

The scent of familiarity catches my nose on a deep inhale—Brent. I can't believe he's here. I never wanted to see him again. Why would I?

The hands on my knees squeeze, and I grimace, knowing who they belong to.

"Please go away." I lace my words with stern conviction despite the fact that my shaking has amped to a scary level.

"Tiger." His muffled words ring through. How dare he use that nickname! He doesn't have that right anymore. He lost that privilege when he walked out on us.

Losing my temper, I tamp down the ill wave that's churning inside, and open my eyes at the same moment I unplug my ears.

As suspected, we've drawn a small crowd. Great. Just great. The jackass is kneeling in front of me, concern written over his otherwise devastatingly handsome face. A face I want to pummel. To spit on. To bloody until all this pent up rage has been expended.

"Tiger." His voice is low, eyes on mine.

I glower in return, then lower my gaze to his hands that haven't moved. To the right, his woman, Vanessa, is standing in shock. Not that I blame her. She doesn't deserve to witness the epic Brent and Katrina showdown. From the screwed up expression on her face, I'd bet she doesn't know who I am. Not that any of these people do. I'm sure I've become a distant memory of his by now. One that he doesn't speak about.

Punching the top of both of his hands, I snarl a shaky, "G-get your fu-cking hands off me, you stupid bastard."

Jeez. I need to generate better comebacks.

If his smirk is any indication, he, too, thinks this is fucking funny. On the other hand, he won't be the one laughing if I get pissed enough to pull out my moves. And by moves, I mean the martial arts my dad taught me as a kid. Being his only child, and a girl, he was determined to make sure that I knew how to protect myself in more ways than one. Not only did I learn multiple forms of martial arts, but I also learned to shoot a gun, which I haven't done in years. And I'm pretty fast with a knife, too. Not that I've had to put any of my training to use in forever. I'm bound to be a bit rusty.

The backs of his hands that remain on my trembling knees are bright red, yet, ever steadfast. I should have known it wouldn't be this easy to make him go away.

I open my mouth to tell him off again. He beats me to it first. "You're shaking, Tiger." His fingers reach up to caress the side of my face. I slap them away.

"Don't touch me!"

"Your blood sugar is low, isn't it?"

He stares at the sweat that drips down the sides of my face. I'm undoubtedly paler than usual. This always happens when my blood sugar drops. The familiar sensation courses through my body. I knew I should have eaten. Then again, I didn't have time to get any food on my way from one side of the Atlanta airport to the next without missing my flight. When it had landed, I didn't think to stop either. I was already running behind, thanks to us sitting on the runway an extra hour because of weather delays.

"I'm fine. I'm just disgusted to see you. I came here to see Bear. Yet, here you are," I snap.

"You need to eat."

He tries for my face again, his expression soft. Almost as if he cares for me. Which is crazy. He's the biggest asshole I've ever met.

Batting him away, I refuse to allow him to touch me any more than he already is.

"Ryker?" Vanessa's voice wavers, and I feel like ten pounds of dog shit.

To grab the situation by the balls, I punch his hands harder this time, to no avail. He still doesn't budge.

"Go away, asshole. Your wife needs you. I'm fine. I just need to see Bear."

Disregarding his woman, Brent's blue eyes capture mine. I look away.

"You shouldn't be here, Tiger."

"You should mind your own damn business."

"And you need to eat. You're sweating. I know your blood sugar is low, Kat. Don't be so damn stubborn."

I hate that he remembers this shit about me. I've had hypoglycemia since I was a kid, and it's always gotten worse when I'm pregnant.

I grit my molars together. "Fuck off. You don't know shit."

"I know that you're gonna be sick soon," he counters softly.

"What about the words, Fuck. Off. don't you understand?"

He sighs. "Listen, I'll grab you something from the kitchen after I help you to your car."

Oh no, he's not. He's not about to tell me what the fuck I'm gonna do by masking it in some generous

36

mensch-like way. I'm not stupid. This is the perfect approach for Sir Asshole himself to forget I was ever here.

A man and woman stand a few feet over, whispering to themselves, pointing at us.

Great. More nosy people.

Refusing to budge or give him the satisfaction of knowing he's right, I tuck my arms over my chest, glancing away from him. "I'm not leaving. I was invited here by Bear. So I'm gonna talk to Bear."

A wave of unease washes over me as I feel my blood sugar plummet. The lightheadedness seizes control, and I close my eyes, taking a deep breath to summon any small fraction of strength I have left before the inevitable ensues.

"What the hell is going on here?" a cumbersome voice interjects. One that's oddly familiar.

Willing my eyes to open as my stomach clenches in pain, I shift my gaze to the right and the man who's stopped dead in his tracks, staring at me slack-jawed.

The eyes I meet are the same ones staring back at me whenever I look in the mirror.

What kinda voodoo shit is this?

One final breath puffs heavily from my lips, I blink, and then the edges of my vision fade to black. My head slumps forward, chin resting on my chest.

He's alive, is the last thought I process before my world fades out and the darkness claims me, rendering me helpless. I welcome it with open arms.

PAST

Setting the grill box on the porch, breathing heavily, sweat glistening on his forehead, my attractive neighbor sighs, running the back of his hand across his face, clearing the wetness. "That should do it." He smiles, all teeth and southern charm. It's stunning. My stomach flutters.

"Thanks." I shift on one foot then the other, trying not to ogle him like I've done from afar for the past two weeks. He just moved into the house next door, and one thing's for sure, he doesn't often wear a shirt outside. Not that you'll hear me complaining. His body's like a Greek sculpture, all sharp lines of molded perfection.

Swallowing, I wash down the drool that threatens to runneth over at the mere thought of his chest and those damn abs. I've never seen a pair this close up before. Not that I'm staring. That would be rude.

He shoots his hand out, pulls it back, wipes it on his jeans, then offers it again. "I'm Brent."

Nerves chewing away at my gut, I force an awkward smile and take his proffered hand. It's firm, yet careful as we shake. A zing shoots up my arm, forcing my heart to thump against my ribs.

"Kat," I reply a little breathily.

"What's that short for?" His palm lingers in mine, softening as if we're on the verge of holding hands. Apprehensively, I jerk mine back and stuff it into my pocket.

Way to act cool, idiot.

"Katrina," I explain.

"Katrina. I like it."

Brent moves to the stairs as I disregard the warm compliment. Stopping on the top step, he glances over his shoulder, his back muscles bunching in stupidly hot ways. I bite my lip to keep from moaning. He's too damn yummy, and I'm a ... I still have my V card. Having an attraction to a man isn't a smart way for me to keep it. Not that he's interested in me. No way is that possible.

"Well, Kat, if you need any more heavy lifting, don't hesitate to ask."

"Thanks. I will," I call after him as he saunters away, his worn leather boots thumping across the sidewalk.

At the edge of our properties, he lifts a hand in a friendly goodbye, and the urge to see him again itches under my skin.

I blurt the first thing that comes to mind. "I'm grilling some steaks tonight if you want one."

Stopping, he turns around and runs his palm down the front of his rippling abs. I squirm at the steady movement. "I'm gonna mow first, then I'll be over." His eyes rake my pitiful yard of yellowing, overgrown grass. It looks more like straw at this point. "How about I do yours, too?"

"You don't have to." Shifting more, I blush ten shades of embarrassment.

"It's not a problem, Kat. You cook, and I'll do the dirty work."

Dirty ... Brent ... *Mmm*...

My mind climbs right back out of the gutter. "Um ... okay ... sure. Thanks."

"No problem. See ya soon." Spinning on his heel, he disappears around the side of his house, and I release a pent up breath.

Crap! Now I have to go to the store and buy some damn steaks. Big ones to feed a man his size, and some potatoes, too. That's what men like him eat, right? I'm way in over my head.

Kicking the box on the porch, grumbling under my breath at the task ahead, I go inside to grab tools to assemble my new grill. Returning to the porch, I gasp as I catch Brent kneeling on it, tearing into the box, pulling out grill parts.

"Figured you might want some help with this first, then I'll mow." He's all smiles, and that single dimple makes my tummy do strange things that it shouldn't be feeling. He's way out of my league. A hammerhead shark would never be interested in a lowly minnow. That's absurd.

Shocked beyond words, I nod like a bobble head doll.

"Great. Here are the instructions." He thrusts them into my hand, and we get to work.

PRESENT

My heavy eyelids pry open as a pressure cuffing around my bicep tightens. *What the heck?* Drearily, I glance over and peel a blood pressure thingy off my arm, tossing it to the floor. On my other arm, there's an IV pumping clear liquid into me from a tall machine a few feet over. By the looks of it, someone raided the hospital.

Grabbing my glasses off the nightstand, I slip them on.

Light from a tall window shines across my sheet-clad legs. Wiggling my toes, I cup my belly, allowing my eyes to adjust to wherever the hell I am. Scanning downward, my eyes fall on the oversized white t-shirt that I'm wearing. My panties are gone. I don't have to inspect myself to know. You can tell. Bare ass on sheets is easily identifiable.

"Don't worry," a husky voice startles me, and I fidget, shifting my wary gaze in the direction of the sound. On the opposite side of the queen bed I'm lying on is a man. A good-looking man with buzzed dark brown hair and blue...

Hey. Wait a minute...

"You're related to the Dickhead, aren't you?" I query for the hell of it, because that same damn crease-like dimple and eyes match Brent's—or whatever his name really is.

Pursing his full lips, he nods. "If you're referring to Ryker, then yeah. I'm his brother, Kade."

Great, a brother. Another thing I never knew about this Ryker fella. Was our entire relationship based on lies? It seems so.

Slipping higher up on the bed, resting my back against the wall, I tuck the sheet around myself, feigning modesty. Not that it matters since I'm mostly undressed. It makes perfect sense that this man has probably seen all my bits by now. Somebody had to have undressed me. However, I'm not one hundred percent sure so let's not take that gamble just in case. Not that it matters, anyhow. Nobody would care if they saw me naked. There's not much to look at. Just ask Bre—Ryker. I'm sure he can fill ya in. Don't worry. It's not that I'm bitter or anything. *Ha.* That's funny. I'm bitter as fuck. And seeing as though I'm in some man's bedroom that smells a whole lot like fabric softener, leather, and cologne, I'm willing to bet that Asshole is somewhere nearby. Or ... that ...

other man... The one with my eyes, nose, and hair. You know, the one that is supposed to be dead, but isn't. My hands ball into fists at the thought. *Lying bastards.*

Deep, angry voices clashing outside the door sever my thoughts, drawing my attention to what lies beyond that oak motherfucker with a silver knob.

"Don't worry about that, either," Kade notes calmly.

I turn my sights back to him.

He does look like his brother. A helluva lot like him. Except he's leaner, younger, and less intimidating in appearance. He's got a friendly face. One that I'm sure slays all the ladies. If he's anything like his brother, he does that regularly.

Massaging my belly, hoping to get a faint kick or two to calm my overwrought nerves, I ask. "So, *Kade*, what's up with me bein' naked, and my father bein' alive?"

Unsure how to act, I cast my sights around the room to preoccupy myself further. Posters of half-naked women litter the walls, and a worn guitar case leans up against a corner. Aside from that, the room's devoid of personality. No family pictures. No trinkets. It's kind of sad.

"Let's just say it's a good thing ya passed out last night when ya did," he remarks, and before I can ask him to elaborate, he pulls a knife out from inside his vest. Expertly flicking the blade open with one hand, he runs it over his wrist like a mental patient, then closes it only to reopen it again to play with the weapon.

What kind of world have I just walked myself into? This is not what I signed up for. None of it.

Sighing exhausted, and shaving hair off his arms with his scary toy, he carries on. "Ryker and your dad got in a fight last night after you passed the fuck out. Vanessa isn't speaking to my brother because you're here. And Bear's pissed that you weren't taken straight to his office when you arrived. Guess, one of the other brothers was supposed to be manning the entrance. But he fucked off to jingle-my-nuts-ville, and Marco took his spot. Of course, that meant Marco didn't know shit about you comin'. *None of us did...*" Contempt clings to his last statement as the blade I can't stop staring at traces the edge of a skull tattoo on his forearm. He pauses a second to collect his thoughts, or I think that's what he's doing...

"Fuck." He tosses his head back, cursing filthier obscenities under his breath. "Listen, Kat." Forcefully, the knife is stabbed into the wall, and I jump, my eyes flying wide as it sinks to the hilt. He doesn't seem to notice, nor care that he's making me uncomfortable. "I'm gonna give it to ya straight." Finally, he looks my way for a response. Scared of my voice squeaking, I nod for him to keep on. Thankfully, he does.

"I didn't know you even fuckin' existed 'til last night." His eyes meet mine for the briefest of seconds, allowing his admission to soak in. It does, to the bitter bone. My stomach turns over, acid surging up my throat. *He never knew I existed.*

"Your dad, Ghost, joined our club fourteen years ago when I was a pimple-faced teenager who thought he was cool as shit. Didn't think nothin' of it. Just like I didn't think nothin' of my big brother leavin' the club to fuck off for a few years. Pop said he went undercover. Then last night, I find out..." Agitated, jaw ticking, he yanks the knife outta the wall and waves it in front of his face, staring deep in thought at the silver tang as light bounces off it, casting designs on the wall.

This is weird. Creepy and weird. I think Asshole's brother needs to see a therapist. And let's not forget the other stuff he just told me. Ghost. That's what they're calling my dad now? Ironic, isn't it? *Ghost*. It's so disturbing that I could almost cry. Hell, all of this makes me want to curl into a ball and sob, all the while wondering how in the fuck my life went from normal, missing my dad like every other girl who loses their father—to this bullcrap. But I won't lose it. I can't. I wasn't raised to be a whiny baby. I'm gonna take any information I can get, and use it to my advantage, just like I was taught. It's better to know all the facts before formulating my plan on how the hell to get out of here. If I wasn't pregnant, I'd climb out the window. Since I am, that idea is nixed. I'm going to have to come up with something better. Something that will get me home to my girls in one piece without wanting to slit my wrists in the process, considering my entire life has just been turned upside down. It's amazing how that happens, isn't it? One second you're coasting along happily in your mundane life, all sunshine and rainbows. Before you know it, your footing slips, and you're forced to adjust to whatever cow shit life tosses in your face. In my case, it seems I've got a father who isn't dead, and an ex who I don't wish to think anything about. So I won't.

A few beats pass before Kade slaps the blade closed, putting it away before he shifts his chair so he's facing me. His biceps, veiled in ink, flex under my scrutiny as his hands perch on his knees. They're rather nice in an entirely objective way.

"I've got two nieces." It's a statement; not a question. I nod, swallowing thickly. "You're the reason my brother has been an insufferable prick for the past eight years or so."

Another declaration that I'm unsure how to respond to, so I don't. I rub my newest daughter instead. A tiny flutter moves in my womb, easing a fraction of my nervousness. At least I know she's okay. Thank God. Honestly, that's all that truly matters. The rest of this drama is trivial. I'm a big girl. I can handle it.

Kade sighs yet again, chewing the corner of his lip. "Listen: I'm really fuckin' sorry about all this." He lifts a hand and waves it around the room like he's projecting the 'this' he's referring to, before returning it to his knee. More noise ensues outside the door. There's a thud as the wall shakes, and the knob audibly rattles.

"Shit!" Kade shoots up from his chair, heading for the door. Standing in front of it like a guard, his posterior blocks any possible intruders.

"I'm going inside!" a man hollers from what I assume is the hallway. There's another loud slam into the wall. Dust wafts into the air, coming off the nudie posters, making me wince.

"The fuck you are! You need to go home, Ryker! Vanessa's already pissed at you!" another man yells.

"We need to talk! I need to speak with her!" Ryker growls, which is trailed by more wall rattling and muffled expletives.

Kade shakes his head, leaning his back against the door, hands stuffed into his front jeans pockets. He's not wearing any socks or shoes, which seems odd considering he's fully clothed.

He notices me regarding his outfit when he remarks. "You're under my protection until further notice." A smile graces his lips for a second, then it's gone the next.

"If I'm not to worry, then why do I need protection?" I ask, eyeing the door as someone attempts to turn the knob. Suddenly, there's a deafening roar followed by a boom that rattles the entire bedroom, including the overhead fan. They must be killing each other out there, and I can't seem to muster any concern about that. Ryker deserves everything that's coming to him, and then some.

Kade grins at the racket. "I knew Pops made the right choice to man the door himself."

"Your dad is the one fighting your brother out there?" Skepticism fills my words. Brent ... Ryker ... whoever he is—he's massive. It'd take a rhinoceros to bring that behemoth to heel.

Kade nods, his grin morphing into an endearing smile. "Yeah. My pops, Bear. He's the only one 'round here who Ryker respects enough *not* to take down.

Pops took that spot last night after he kicked Ghost outta the clubhouse for tryin' to start more shit."

"What kinda shit?"

You'd think that my gut instinct would warn me to protect myself since I'm trapped in a room, half naked with a biker, as pigheaded men wrestle in the hall. Yet, it's as quiet as a church mouse. Either my gut radar has short-circuited, or it's on board with the rest of my senses. Which are telling me that Kade is one of the good guys. Aside from Ryker, I've always been a decent judge of character. And from the way Kade regards me with compassion, I'd say I'm on the mark. So, like he said, there's nothing imminent to worry about. At least not where my body is concerned. Now, my mind, on the other hand, is a whole different can of worms.

Kade opens his mouth to answer at the same time a sharp knock sounds at the door. "It's me," the man on the other side sputters, breathless.

"Did he leave?" Kade doesn't move an inch as he waits for a reply.

"Yeah. The stubborn fucker left. Both of 'em are gone for now. But, they'll both be back for dinner."

Dinner... Wha—Duh. Today's Thanksgiving. I almost forgot. I've gotta call my girls soon to wish them a Happy Turkey Day. I'm sure they're driving my mother crazy by now, trying to help her cook. Scarlett, my eight-year-old, is a quick learner in the kitchen. Roxie, my nine-year-old ... not so much. She still has issues pouring milk into her cereal bowl without spilling it all over the counter and down the front of the cabinets.

Kade steps away from the door and turns the handle, pulling it open. The man who I've seen one picture of takes up the entire frame, before shuffling sluggishly into the room. Not seeking an invitation, he plops down on the edge of the bed a few inches from where my toes reach. A crooked smile graces his lips as he turns his attention my way and pats the top of my sheeted legs. Exhaling a breath I didn't know I was holding, I relax beneath his compassionate touch.

"I'm Bear," he huffs, still attempting to catch his breath.

Running fingers through my bedhead, I smirk. "I've seen what you look like. Haven't changed much from your picture." Except his beard has grown a few inches, and he's even bigger in person than I thought. No wonder Bre—Ryker is so large. He must take after his dad. Shit. I still can't believe he *is* his dad. The Brent I knew said his parents were dead. Another lie fed to me from the devil himself.

Observing me for a moment, his gaze rakes me from top to bottom in a tender fashion before returning to meet my eyes. He scratches his beard, and Kade shuts the door, resuming his guard station. With his back pressed against the wood, Kade's hands tuck into his front pockets, face impassive. He looks kinda cool in a lethal, badass sort of way.

"I'm gonna cut to the chase." Bear raises a brow as if he's challenging me to protest. It's not going to happen. I like straight shooters.

"Okay," I mutter.

"I didn't know jack about your website post. It was a lucky guess..." He sighs just like Kade does. "To make a long fuckin' story short, I'm tired of dealin' with Ryker's bullshit, and Ghost bein' a sullen baby all the damn time because of you."

My hackles rise, and I sit up straighter, eyes narrowing. "What the hell did I do?"

Bear waves off my words with the flick of his wrist. "Now don't get all pissy with me, darlin'. I've got enough emotional baggage I gotta deal with from them. I'm not sayin' it's your *fault*. It's not. But Ghost made his damn bed, just as Ryker did."

Keep a tight leash on your emotions, Kat.

"What's that supposed to mean?"

He pats my leg again, and I relax as if his touch is flippin' magic or something. It seems that way. "The past twenty-four hours have gone to shit, darlin'. I'd planned on meetin' up with ya, explainin' all this, then lettin' ya see both of the men to get some closure. That didn't fuckin' happen. So, now I've got a pissed off son, an even angrier VP, and a daughter-in-law ready to put my son's nuts in a vice."

Secretly, I hope she does, and cackle internally at the thought. Maybe that'll teach the jerk a lesson or two. Go, Vanessa. I like her already.

"Listen," I start.

Warily, I reach out and pat his shoulder to offer a little comfort, letting him know there're no hard feelings from my end. Shit happens. I'm not actually angry. I was stupid enough to come here in the first place. Then, I passed out from blood sugar problems. They've taken care of me. Albeit, I wish my clothes were still on; but I'm safe, and Kade seems like a decent protector. Not that I actually need one of those. But whatever.

I continue, "I'm tryin' not to lose my shit, okay. Thinkin' I'm coming here to find out stuff about my dad is one thing. Finding him alive is another. On top of that, my ex is here with a wife. An ex I haven't seen in m—years, and is also the father of my daughters. Sorry, Bear. I'm doin' the best I can to keep a fuckin' lid on my emotions. But you gotta start fillin' in the blanks. All of 'em. And fast."

Bear turns his sights on his son, who's watching us. "I like her." He thumbs in my direction, talking as if I'm not present. I can't lie. His little admission warms my belly, and I smother the smile that tries to quirk. Now is the time to remain impassive.

Kade bobs his head, eyes on his father, smirking like the cat who swallowed the canary. "Yup. She's somethin'."

Another flitter of heat joins the first.

Shifting on the bed, hooking part of his leg onto the mattress so he's facing me, Bear gets comfortable. "First, I think ya need to know your dad was in a bad way when the Sacred Sinners mother chapter, up by y'all, decided to put him under our form of witness protection."

"Is that why you faked his death?" I ask.

"Yup. Big Dick, our national prez, sent him to us right after it all went down. Sorry. I can't tell ya much more. That's club business, and I'm not authorized to tell ya. Hell. You're not even supposed to know he's still kickin'." He scrubs his long graying beard. "And ya wouldn't know if it weren't for my son screwin' up a simple prospecting duty."

Now that tidbit has captured my attention more than my father's mess—his, I kinda subconsciously suspected. This, not so much. I guess that's what I get for sleuthing the past umpteen years, trying to get some headway into my father's untimely demise. Faking his death seems more logical now that I think about it. Especially after the report went missing. Not sure why I didn't consider it before. Guess that's one of the reasons I'm not a cop. I suck at finding out stuff.

"Keep going," I urge impatiently, and he chuckles, shaking his head, wearing a lopsided grin.

"I really like you," he praises before keepin' on, and I pretend my internal warmth didn't just triple. "We caught wind of ya movin' back home from Vegas, and my son was chompin' at the bit to cut his prospecting time in half."

"What's prospecting?"

Hey. Don't judge me. I don't know a damn thing about this motorcycle club stuff, and I'm piecing tidbits together as I go along. You would be, too, if you were in my shoes.

"When ya wanna join a club, ya gotta put in the time. Do grunt work. Show your loyalty. Shit like that," Bear answers patiently.

"Okay. So Bre—Ryker wanted to make this trial period go faster?" Rubbing my belly in tiny circles with both hands, I wait for another flutter or two to sharpen my objective thinking. I can't dissect the potential ramifications of what I'm about to find out, and listen at the same time. That's another thing my daddy taught me. Listen first, dissect later.

Bear nods, still flashing me that lopsided grin like he's tickled with me. I like it. I like it a lot. In front of the door, Kade, with his strong presence, raptly observes our exchange. "Right. So Ghost decided we'd put him on a three-month trial period. Send him up to you. Let him do some surveillance. Standard club stuff. Basically, easy work that we have to order somebody else do—"

"He wasn't supposed to be my friend, was he?" I cut in.

Bear shakes his head, pressing his lips together, jaw ticking. "No. He wasn't." His tone is stern. "He wasn't supposed to even talk to you. When we found out you were *friends,* I demanded he come home. The stubborn son of a bitch ignored me, and a week later, told us you were pregnant."

"So I was a job?" I blurt, aching at the thought.

Of course, I was a job. There's no way a hot guy like him would magically move in next door and want to spend time with me. Sure, that doesn't change the fact that he befriended me when he wasn't supposed to. But the outcome is much the same. My daughters growing up without a father as I mourn his loss alongside my own dad's death. It's sick and depressive, wrapped into a big ball of suck.

"No," Bear grumbles at the same moment Kade says, "Yes."

Swapping scowls between the both of them, I move anxiously on the bed, itching to walk right out of this place and never look back. I've stayed calm.

53

I've heard what I needed to hear. I've been objective and done what I was taught. Yet, this is all I've learned—people really enjoy fucking with my life as if it means jack shit to them. Bear wanted me to come here so he could give me closure. As if seeing my dad would give me any. I thought he was already dead. What other kind of closure do you really need? One that says he's fucking alive, and I can't see him ever again? Are you shitting me? Or how about the fact that my children's father was sent to spy on me. For what? I don't know. Probably something to do with more of this phony-bologna club business that they won't tell me, anyhow. So now I'm supposed to just sit here, digest all of this like a good little girl? Then what? Go home and forget this ever happened? There's no way I can do that. No fucking way.

My temper blazes, revving my heart into overdrive. Blood rushes through my ears. "You're saying I was a job? And that you want me, or them to get closure? I'm confused as hell. This makes no sense to me. You put my dad in this MC witness protection bullshit, let me live without him for more than half my life, and now you want me to see him again? Why now? Why not then?" I shake my head, unable to wrap anything around it. "You're not making a damn bit of sense. Except for telling me why he's here, and that your lying-sack-of-dog-shit son only got with me out of convenience, or whatever you call it." Reflexively, I cross my arms over my substantial chest to show I mean business. He better not jerk me around. I don't have an ounce of patience left. Not when I know for a fact he's not giving up all the goods. My dad going under this protection thingy makes sense, sure. But, suddenly wanting him to see me doesn't.

Sighing long and hard, Bear runs a palm over the top of his head. "I had a heart attack three months ago," he says as if it's the magical explanation to all of this idiocy. "It gave me a new outlook on life and the shit that really matters. My sons and the club matter. My grandkids matter. My VP matters." He meets my gaze, an air of sadness floating between us. "I made Ryker leave ya all those years ago because I thought I was teachin' him a lesson..."

Dropping his eyes to his lap, looking awfully guilty, he continues. "I'm not the best kinda man. I've made some bad choices in life. Sendin' Ryker up there to do surveillance on ya wasn't right to begin with. Then, to allow him to sow his wild oats with ya was even more fucked. 'Cause every time I turned around, he was knockin' ya up. Lookin' back now, I see he only did it so he could stay there longer, 'cause he knew I wasn't gonna make him come home when you were pregnant. After Scarlett was born, bein' the prick that I am, I gave him an ultimatum. Told him he'd better come home, or he'd be out of the club. He had to choose. The club, or you three."

The acrid taste of bitterness bathes my tongue. "Ryker chose you over his daughters and me. I get it." My venom drifts into the air, potent and lethal.

How fucking dare they do that! How fucking dare *he*! I don't care who your father is. Or your brother. None of it. You choose your kids, always and forever. They are what carries your legacy through generations. They are the future. What is wrong with these men? What is wrong with Ryker?

"My brother was a jackass," Kade interjects, looking mighty pissed as he stands up straighter, his knife back out, blade tracing more of those tattoos on his arms without breaking the skin.

"I'm the jackass," Bear counters. "I've felt like shit for years over what ya must've been goin' through with your pops. Then Ryker goes and fucks ya over even more. I do have a heart. It's not very big. But it does beat, and I do feel things. Not much. But I've felt this. A whole ocean of guilt. So, one day I decided to look ya up on *Facebook*. Next thing I knew, I was emailin' ya." Finally, he lifts his head and meets my eyes once more. I want to look away to be a bitch, but can't. The pain in his voice tells me that he's trying. I'm a sucker for broken men, and never said I was smart. "The fact of the matter is, darlin', I wanna make some sort of amends. I wanna know my grandbabies before I die. I'm not gettin' any younger. And I knew I couldn't see them without givin' Ghost the opportunity to get to know more about 'em, too. Since we're both their grandpas. I don't care how angry ya are about all this. You're entitled to it. Fuck. I'd be stark ravin' mad if I were you—"

"I'm not that kind of person," I interrupt.

"You're a better person than I'll ever be."

Jesus. I hate to say this, but the sorrow coming off him in waves is stifling. I wanna give the guy a big hug just so he'll stop killing my heart with all that anguish. He's a lot more emotional than he thinks. His expressions show it all. Every ounce of turmoil, every spark of happiness, every flutter of hope. Ryker is a lot like him in that way; he was never able to hide his feelings from me, because they're right there for all to see. Some might view that as weakness. I feel that it's an admirable strength to be able to wear your emotions on your proverbial sleeve and not give two shits what others think about it. Sometimes, I wish I had that much courage. I don't. Not by a long shot. I've got what you'd call the 'mom face'. I keep it all in, level and unemotional, until I feel the need to express a sentiment. It helps that I've had years worth of practice.

"Why don't I have a daddy?" is Scarlett's new question that guts me. So I school my features instead of having a meltdown in my daughter's arms. I don't fill her with fatherly hope or colorful dreams of the knight-in-shining-armor he could be. No. I give it to her straight. The detached truth that she was given a mommy who was capable of playing both mom and dad. And that sometimes kids aren't blessed with two parents. I don't tell them how he vanished. They don't even know what he looks like. I keep those few pictures hidden in a box under my bed where they'll never find them. For all intents and purposes, Brent/Ryker, whoever he may be, does not exist in our lives. It's not fair to my girls to place him there. Sadly, I know a bit of what they're going through; what it feels like every time a dad brings their daughter to school or proudly attends their dance recitals. I felt it every time I saw a mother and daughter doing things together. Painting nails. Going shopping. I never had any of that either. My mom left

me with my dad. He was all I needed. The one who learned to braid hair, teach me about female hygiene, and all of those other things moms are supposed to impart. Sure, my grandma was there to help guide him. But he did most of it on his own, in a way only a man can. I'd always hoped that my daughters wouldn't have to experience what I did growing up. Unfortunately, history has somewhat repeated itself. If I could have changed that, I would've. Brent made it impossible. I guess that's what I get for falling in love with the boy next door who shattered my heart into a billion pieces. On the bright side, though, I'm stronger for it. Nobody can hurt me like that ever again. Not when I refuse to give anyone that kind of power over my life.

A pregnant silence settles over the room as we sit and stare at each other, exchanging gazes from one person to the next. Not that there's much to take in. Kade is, of course, upset. 'Cause, like his dad and brother, his scowling tells an animated story of how unhappy he truly is. If that wasn't indication enough, the blade in his hand, and the eye twitch is a dead giveaway. Bear, though, is a big gooey ball of sadness. It seeps from his pores, perfuming the air in melancholy. I'm depressed just from looking at him. Poor guy.

To keep things upbeat, and stave off any further self-flagellation, I take the high road and do what I do best—focus on the positives. I am an optimist after all. Except where the behemoth Asshole is concerned.

"Okay, guys, no more of this sullen crap. It's Thanksgiving. Don't you do anything special for the holiday?" My goal was to be at my hotel by now. I had zero plans to spend Thanksgiving anywhere, especially here. Yes. I know I could have flown home today and spent a late Turkey Day with my kids. But I didn't want to fly in one day and fly out again less than twelve hours later. My pregnant body can't handle that. The water retention I have is real, and flying only makes it worse—much worse. I haven't scoped them out yet, but I'm willing to bet my ankles look like honey glazed hams. Oh, the wonderful joys of motherhood.

"Some of the old ladies are cookin'," Kade explains, flipping his knife shut and stowing it back inside his vest. I'm happy to see it disappear.

"That sounds great." I go for cheerful to draw the attention away from the sour fog that's descended upon the room, and is growing denser by the minute.

"You're too fuckin' nice," Bear mumbles. "You should be yellin' at me and sayin' I can never see my grandbabies for the shit I've put ya through."

"You didn't put me through anything," I argue gently.

"Sure I did." More of that negativity imbues the air. Soon, we're going to be choking on it. It's got to stop. It's Thanksgiving, for cryin' out loud.

"How? By takin' my dad in for the poor choices he made, or giving Bre—Ryker an ultimatum when you thought it was in his best interest? I'm a mom. As parents, we don't always make the right choices, but we do our best. And I'm old enough to know not to direct my anger toward someone undeserving. Ryker made his choice, as you said. So did my dad. And I'm not going to punish you, or Kade, for their piss poor decisions."

"Pops, I told ya she wasn't gonna act like a crazy bitch," Kade interjects, grinning proudly in my direction. It's so warm that I want to puff my chest up at the compliment, but I've got to pee so badly all of a sudden that I can't see straight.

I wiggle in my spot, ready to burst. "Um ... guys ... can I use the restroom? I've got an iron bladder, but bein' pregnant kinda interferes with my self-proclaimed bladder awesomeness."

They both chuckle as Kade saunters across the room and pushes open a door. "It's all yours." Suavely, he sweeps his hand toward the darkened interior like Vanna White.

Raising my arm, I remind him of my IV. Nodding, Kade walks over to my bedside. Turning off the machine, he grabs some white gauze and tape from the bedside drawer, then, bingo-bango, the IV comes out, and I'm all patched up. Not a drop of blood spilled. Something tells me he's done this plenty of times before.

Shoving the sheet down my legs, I voice a quick thanks and make haste to the bathroom while securing the hem of the t-shirt. Luckily, it almost reaches my knees. I don't need to give these men a nudie show. The bedroom walls can provide them with enough flesh entertainment for one evening.

Flicking the light on, the stark white-on-white bathroom is cleaner than I suspected since it's used by a man. Most of the fellas I know are slobs. Cologne and other manly items are neatly laid out on the counter as a blue towel hangs on a bar a few feet from the toilet.

I shut the door.

Voices in the other room draw my attention as I lift my shirt to use the facilities.

"She doesn't hate us, Pop," Kade states.

"She should. She came here under false pretenses. Now Ryker's gonna wanna talk to her, and Ghost is gonna kill him."

"Do ya blame him?"

Leaning forward a little, elbows perched on my knees, I strain to listen.

"No. If I were Ghost, I'd hate him, too, for leavin' that poor woman, and her two daughters," Bear remarks.

"Yeah. But that's a choice *he* made. You did what any good prez would do. Made him choose—club or woman. He showed his loyalty to the club just like you would've done. What'd ya expect him to do? We were raised in this life. It ain't like we're gonna pass it up for some chick. That's disloyal to the patch."

It's sad how much conviction Kade places into his words. *Pass it up for some chick.* That's a bit harsh, don't ya think? I'm not just some woman.

"Ghost doesn't see it that way. He was taken away from his daughter because of his foolish shit. He wasn't brought up like y'all. Big did right by him. By helpin' him out. But the man wasn't raised an outlaw. He just served us from the outside. That girl is all that's ever mattered to him." Bear speaks with reason, and I nod along, agreeing with him the entire way. Not that I'm defending my dad. But when I was

61

a kid, I was his priority. His pride and joy. I knew that then, and I know that even more so now.

"That's why you've kept tabs on her like you promised ya would. So he'd keep the heat off the club. You did all that was expected," Kade defends his father's honor. It's kinda sweet.

Finished, I remain on the toilet to eavesdrop more than I probably should. Hey, you gotta do what ya gotta do. And you're joinin' me, so what does that say about you?

"Can you tell me why she's wearin' one of your shirts, son?" There's a smile in Bear's voice.

Lifting the shirt edge to my nose, I inhale deeply and nearly groan at the subtle masculine scent that clings to the cotton. The spicy smell of man is one of my biggest weaknesses. Not that I have many. Unfortunately, or fortunately, depending on how you look at it, Kade smells amazing. It doesn't hurt that he's a looker, too.

Damn it. I can't be ogling my ex's brother—the uncle to my kids. That's low, even for me—the born again virgin. Okay, so I'm not a born-again anything. I've just been celibate for so long that I've forgotten what it feels like to be touched down there. And I'm sure you're wondering ... *Don't ya have a dildo or vibrator, Kat?* The answer would be no. Not anymore. When Roxie was about three, she snuck into my bedside drawer and decided to play with my pink vibrator like it was a neck massager. I then threw out all sexual paraphernalia from my home just to be on the safe side. At their ages now, they'd recognize what those things are.

It's sad that kids know more about sex at age nine than I did. Aren't they still supposed to be playing *Barbie*s and dressing up like princesses? Where does the time go? Am I right? Now all they want to do is play games on their tablets, cruise *YouTube*, and dance. At least I've convinced them to take part in one extracurricular activity that doesn't involve the internet, or, more specifically, *Facebook*. Which is another thing they've been begging me for—a *Facebook* page. Which is not gonna happen until they're a hundred and five years old. Mama has to put her foot down on that one.

"Those fuckers got blood on her during their fight. What was I supposed to do?" Kade growls defensively.

"Not undress her," Bear clips as I flush the toilet and thoroughly wash my hands in the sink to buy them more time to talk.

Giving myself a once over in the mirror makes me feel grimy. So I refuse to let my gaze linger any longer than is necessary on my unfortunate state—that's complete with messy hair and bags under my eyes. Upon further inspection, I notice that my ankles are, indeed, basking in all of their plump, hoggish-glory while my toes and feet have decided to party right along with them. Oh, joy. It's going to be interesting to see if I can fit my feet into one of the two pairs of flats that I brought. I probably should have planned better and packed my slippers. They would've fit for sure.

"I've been trained to handle this kinda stuff, Pops. Remember?" I hear Kade argue as I open the bathroom door and make my way back to the bed, sliding under the covers.

The men stop talking, and their eyes train on me as if I have something important to say. I don't. There's not much *to* say. I'm honestly not sure where to go from here. Shock would be an appropriate term at this juncture. What can I really do? I'm at their mercy unless I want to leave. And I don't want to. I have so much more I'd like to find out. Plus, speak to my dad if I can.

Now that sounds strange to me. *Speak to my dad.* As if that was something I could do outside of my head. Like when I used to pray, night after night, that he would hear the stories I whispered to him about the girls, missing him and our family. Stories that now make me sound like a lunatic since nobody was listening.

"Dinner should be done 'round seven," Bear finally speaks, now standing by the door as Kade retakes his seat on the opposite side of the bed. His hand wraps around the knob. "I'd like it if you'd join us."

My eyes snap down to my shirt and back again. "What am I gonna wear?"

Bear's attention sweeps to Kade as he inclines his head in his son's direction. "He's the one who'll look after ya, and get ya what ya need."

"Am I going to be allowed to go to my hotel tonight?"

"No. We've already canceled your stay. Kade's room is the safest place for ya."

"Am I in danger?" I sincerely hope not.

Bear shakes his head, scratching at his beard. "Not danger. But you're new 'round here. People know you're Ghost's daughter. And unless you wanna have a run-in with Vanessa or Ryker unaccompanied, then I suggest ya stay put and listen to Kade. You can trust him. He's a good man. Won't let anyone give ya any shit."

I look to Kade, and he proudly lifts his chin, confirming what his dad said is true. "Okay. So am I a ... prisoner?"

"No!" they blurt in unison as if I offended them.

"Am I gonna be able to leave tomorrow to go back home?"

Apparently, I'm full of questions.

"With an escort ya can," Bear explains.

Not wanting to think about *why* I have to have an escort, I nod my head in acquiesce. Not like I have much of a choice. Do I? As long as I get home safe and sound, that's all that matters.

Bear exits, but not before he bows his head in goodbye, leaving me alone with Kade once more.

Shifting on the mattress, I face him. "I'll need my clothes and phone."

"I can't give ya your phone."

Oh. That's not gonna fly.

"Care to tell me why?"

I remain calm, even if my temper is starting to rise. I'm going to give him one more chance to make the right choice, or the mouthy part of me will be unleashed. This time, I don't care one bit. Those are my daughters, and I'll be damned if anyone keeps me

65

from talking to them. Especially on a national holiday.

"Can't risk it. Your line's not secure," he clarifies, his attention focused my way, casually lounging in the chair. At least his knife isn't out.

My arms do their thing, tucking over my chest like I'm preparing for a fight. Cocking my head to the side, my lips thin with agitation. "Then I suggest you find me a phone that is, because I am going to call my daughters whether you like it or not."

That seems to perk him right up.

"You're gonna call Scarlett and Roxie?"

"Yes. Genius. Those *are* my daughters," I tease, releasing my arms from their tense state so I can rub my belly instead. It's starting to growl. I'm starving. Low blood sugar curbed or not, I haven't eaten in nearly twenty-four hours. My body is starting to punish me for it.

Kade smirks and pulls a phone from his back pocket. Dangling it from his fingertips over the edge of the bed, he delivers his ultimatum. "I'll let ya call them from my cell. The number is untraceable. But ya gotta put it on speaker phone."

"Why would I do that?"

"So I can hear what my nieces sound like."

Awe. Now that's just too damn sweet. Who could say no to that? Not me. Particularly not when his face is lax and adorable. Lips soft. Eyes gentle. Everything about him is open, waiting, and hoping. Telling him 'no' would be like kicking a puppy; although, he'd probably take the kick with grace and still let me use his phone. He's just that kinda guy. Or seems to be.

"Okay," I agree. He doesn't waste any time to dial my mother's number, which he shouldn't know, before laying the ringing phone on the bed, speaker on.

"Hello?" she answers.

"Hey, Mom. It's me."

"Kat? Why are you calling me from a restricted number?" Her voice jumps a few octaves.

The first lie I can muster drops effortlessly from my lips. "No signal out here in the boonies. I'm using one of the members' phones."

See, not a total untruth.

"Are you being safe?"

There she goes trying to act motherly. When she never cared about that before when I was young enough to actually need mothering. It gets under my skin more than it should. I know this. But I can't lie and say I don't still hold some animosity toward her because of my childhood. The past few years have significantly lessened some of the resentment. Even though it's still very much intact. Friendship with her is something that I can do. Having her act like a concerned mother ... not so much. It's all in her tone. Shelly's friend tone is chill and approachable. Her mom tone is snappy, borderline demanding. It's never pleasant, and, thankfully, it rarely comes out. She means well regardless. I'm trying to see that. Still, it's hard when you've pictured her one way for more than half your life. As much of an optimist as I am, that doesn't change the baggage that I carry. It's heavy and weighed down by a weathered past. Unfortunately, my mom has to bear the brunt of that sometimes. I'm getting better. Repressing feelings works wonders for me. I tuck them into tiny compartmentalized boxes and pretend they don't exist. That way, I don't have to work them out. It's a magical method, even if it's not the healthiest. What can I say? You don't get the luxury of ironing all of your emotional crap when you're a mom. Kids come first.

"I'm fine. Are the girls around?" I look up to see Kade staring at the phone like it's a precious gem. He's hunched over, elbows on knees, less than a foot from it. His breath puffs sharp enough that it fogs the edge of the screen.

Mom grumbles into the receiver, apparently not fond of my response. "Yes. Hold on. They're out back playing."

There's some yelling and rustling on the other line as I hear Mom calling to the girls, telling them I'm waiting to talk. Roxie is the first to snatch the phone. She's the more eager of the two. "Mommy!" She takes a long pause to pant for breath. It abrades the speaker with noise. "Hi, Mommy! Are you having fun in Texas?"

Another glance toward Kade, and I swear my ovaries explode. He's smiling hugely at the phone, not even noticing me watching him. He's too enraptured with the little girl on the line that he's oblivious to everything else. It's so damn cute. I almost "awe" aloud, but swallow the sound at the last second, not wanting to draw his attention away.

"Mommy!" Roxie screeches, transporting me back to the present.

"Hey, Rox. Texas is great. A lot warmer here than back home." I always keep my tone light with my kids to keep them from worrying about me.

"We got snow. Grandma is letting us play in it while she cooks."

"That sounds fun. Are you wearing your new gloves?"

"Yessss, Mom," she whines playfully, a giggle lingering under breath. I adore this little girl so damn much my heart could almost burst.

Delicately, I touch my chest, grinning like a proud mama. "Happy Thanksgiving, babes. Have fun. I won't keep ya. Can I talk to Scarlett?"

"Sure. Love you!" Her enthusiasm ricochets off the bedroom walls.

"Love you, too, sweetie."

The phone is passed to Scarlett, and the same conversation ensues like it always does. We say our *love yous*, and they hang up before my mom can return to the phone. I'm better for it since I know she'll want to ask another fifty questions. Today's not the day for me to answer them.

Returning his phone to his pocket, a hardy slice of silence descends upon us, as our eyes awkwardly roam each other and the room, never stopping on any one thing for too long.

A few minutes pass before I can't take the quiet any longer. It's making my skin crawl. "So how many live in this place?" I inquire because I can't think of anything else to ask that wouldn't be intrusive. Like, how long has your brother been married? Not that I really care. Is my dad seeing anyone? Does he have any other kids? How does your wife feel about me staying in your room? Not that I need or want to know that either. Ya know, for anything more than polite conversation, and so I don't have to worry about some jealous woman wanting to try to kick my pregnant ass. Not that I've had many of those to deal with in my life, because I haven't.

Kade appears deep in thought for a beat, scratching his prickly chin—like father, like son. "Ten to twelve of us. Dependin' on the week."

"Does it bother you that I'm here, and you're playin' babysitter?"

This is something I need to know. Being a burden to anyone bothers me. Even when it pertains to my mother. I've always been independent. I haven't had much of a choice with the life I've had. Dads can only do so much when they have to work. I was left home alone, a lot. Then, when I moved to Vegas with my mom, she was rarely present. It was always work or her boyfriend that took precedence. Sure, the first few months after my father's alleged death she tried to be a doting mother. That lasted all of two seconds before our distant relationship reemerged. I spent most of my time reading. Hence, the reason I'm a librarian. Though, if I had it my way, I'd be a copy editor or something more fantastical like an actual author. Not that I have the ability to write anything more than a shopping list as creativity isn't exactly my forte.

Kade's nose crinkles in repugnance. "Fuck no, it doesn't bother me. What pisses me off is that I'm just findin' out about you and my nieces. And ever since last night, I keep wonderin' what I can do to help ya. Even after ya leave here."

He's a good man. I knew my gut was right. That's one of the sweetest, most selfless things anyone has ever said to me.

"We do fine on our own, Kade. You don't gotta worry about us." I try for sincere reassurance. Granted, I think it comes out half-assed because I'm hungry and still pretty tired.

Those stern eyes meet mine, pinched between the brow. The corded muscles in his neck flex. It would be kinda sexy in its own way if he weren't so pissed off. "You're not okay, Kat. Your dad fucks ya over. My brother fucks ya over. And it takes my pops havin' to have a goddamn heart attack to even give two shits about you. That's the furthest from okay. I'm not a nice guy. I've done a fuckuva lot of illegal shit. Hurt people without battin' an eyelash. I'm an outlaw. Proud of it, too. But I was raised to respect all women. Even the club whores. I always lick their pussies 'til they come. Then I get mine..."

Sweet Mary, mother of God, I can't believe he's saying this stuff to me! I'm not fragile by any means, but I've never had a man, aside from Brent, speak so candidly about sex. Even though, I do it myself quite often. It's driven all of my exes nuts. Well, that, and the fact that I wouldn't have sex with them. Except Asshole, obviously.

He keeps on, "So what I'm sayin' is: you don't know me. I don't know you. But you're never gonna be a burden to me. We're family, so I've got your back. Tonight, when we go down to the party, there's

71

gonna be a fuckuva lot of tension. And a lot of people starin', waitin' for Ghost and Ryker to finish what they started last night before Pops and I peeled them off each other."

I arch a brow. "It was that bad?"

He nods firmly. "Real fuckin' bad. They pulled out their knives. I ended up havin' to stitch both of their dumbasses."

"Are you a doctor?"

"Not exactly."

He's evasive, and I'm having none of that.

"Are ya gonna tell me what you are, then? Or am I gonna have to guess? Because I don't think you wanna hear my theory of you bein' abducted by aliens and implanted with a super smart bug just so you can help pregnant women who pass out from low blood sugar."

Just as I was intending, he throws his head back and laughs. It's a beautiful, booming sound that hits me in my chest, making me happier than I've been in a long time.

There's a knock at the door. "You better not be fuckin' the guest in there, Kade!" a male hollers good-naturedly.

"Fuck off, Creeper!" Kade half yells, half laughs, scrubbing the side of his cheek with his palm, smiling brightly—all teeth and sexiness. Women have to swoon at his feet. He's just too damn handsome for his own good. Well, so is his brother. On the other hand Bre—Ryker knows how attractive he is, whereas Kade seems humble about it. It's an endearing quality.

"Bear said you need to feed her more than your puny dick. So get your horny asses dressed and come down and grab some grub," the man adds.

Inquisitive, I wanna ask if the club thinks we're sleeping together since we've been holed up here for a while. However, before the thought passes completely through my brain, Kade is standing up and plopping himself closer to me on the bed. It dips as he takes a spot against the wall, feet up, our shoulders inches from touching. His heady scent drifts into my nose and burrows there, making certain female parts way too pleased. I squirm a little, mostly on the inside, but a little on the outside, too. The warmth of him is like a magnet. I want to press closer, but don't.

"Ignore Creeper. He's just a pest. Nobody thinks I'm feedin' ya my dick," he reassures, unamused.

"Good, 'cause I hear it's puny. And I'm partial to monster cocks. Or didn't ya know?" I deadpan, pressing my lips together to keep from smiling. Even if my eyes give my amusement away.

Another one of his charming laughs is music to my ears as Creeper, who apparently hasn't left, yells through the door another time. "Get dressed, you horny fucker! Janet is comin' tonight. You gotta save up a load or two. And ya know Ryker and Ghost will be out for blood if you bring her to dinner with cum stains on her pants."

"Will you cut it out?!" Exasperated, Kade shakes his head, amusement a thing of the past. Out of the corner of my eye, I catch him balling and un-balling his fists in his lap. His knuckles drain of color, white pinching through as he clenches, then the tanned creaminess returns as he allows the blood to rush back in. Over and over, he does this as a low grumble percolates in his throat, sounding a whole lot like Brent when he was angry.

Knowing I have to cut the irritation off at the pass before he gets carried away, I do what I do best and blurt the first idiocy that comes to mind.

"Don't worry, Creeper," I speak loud enough so I know he'll hear. "I'll be sure to wear fresh clothes when we come down. Wouldn't want the cum stains to make everyone jealous."

There's a bark of laughter coming from the hallway as a smaller one rumbles beside me.

"She's got jokes!" Creeper cheers.

"Careful, or he'll be proposing marriage by dinner," Kade teases in a whisper. His powerful hands flatten on the top of his thighs as his long, thick fingers fan outward.

"I'm not worried." Cheerfully, I bump my shoulder into his.

He seems to ignore my friendly gesture when he shouts, "We'll be down soon! Tell Pops to chill!"

"Ya know he's just worried that she won't come out. That's why he sent me up here." Creeper's tone is no longer full of fun and games. It's all business. I like it better the other way.

"I know. But he's worryin' about somethin' he shouldn't," Kade declares.

"Okay. If you're sure. 'Cause I'm under orders not to move until ya go get her clothes."

"They're already in my closet. I got 'em last night. I'll let her get washed or whatever she wants. Then we'll be down. You're actin' like a bunch of mother-hen bitches. We've had plenty of pregnant chicks in the clubhouse before." Kade's losing his patience again.

"Not one that's family," Creeper replies, delivering a swift punch of marshmallowy joy to my soul. *Family.*

Curiosity digs, clawing in deeper, and I open my mouth to ask more questions about this so called family, but stop myself when Creeper says, "Later."

Kade silently climbs off the bed, snatching my bag out of his closet. "Sorry. I forgot to tell ya 'bout it earlier. Last night, I undressed ya 'cause there was a shit ton of blood on your clothes. Even on your underwear and bra. I had to throw 'em out. Didn't wanna have to wrestle your unconscious body any more than I had to, so I slipped ya into one of my shirts. I promise I dressed you with dignity, and didn't cop a single feel," he rambles timidly with his head bowed, shielding his eyes as he sets my ancient duffle on the bed beside me. It's the same bag my dad used to go on trips with. An oversized blue one with frayed handles and a hole in the bottom that I've had to patch four times. My mom gives me crap every time I use it. But it's tradition, and I'm not about to break that for some fancy suitcase on wheels. Even if my back could use the relief.

Grabbing the handle of my duffel, I yank it onto my lap, then pat the spot it vacated, hating the almost vulnerable way Kade is acting. The men in this family are way more emotional than any I've ever met before. When he doesn't budge to rejoin me on the bed, I pat the cold spot once more. "I'm fine. We're fine." My tone is easy. "I've given birth to two children, Kade. My body isn't a wonderland any more. It's a battlefield. You seein' me nude, which may not be ideal, doesn't mean I'm angry about it. Do you realize how many people have seen me naked in my lifetime? A man taking care of me when I'm unconscious isn't gonna be the end of my world." My voice succeeds at delivering my peaceful speech, while my brain is screaming in horror at the mere thought of him seeing all of this ickiness unclothed. I can't imagine the disgusted faces he probably made while performing his duty. It's a damn good thing I was unconscious, so I didn't get to see them. It wouldn't be the first or last time a man has been repulsed by my stretch marks, overly broad hips, or breasts that are not as perky as they once were.

Instead of glancing my way or responding to what I said, Kade walks over to his bathroom door and reaches inside to flip the light on. "You can take a shower whenever you're ready. There are towels under the sink. I grabbed a new bar of soap for ya to use so you won't be forced to use my body wash. We'll head down to grab ya a bite after you've finished." Stepping away from the illuminated doorway, Kade returns to his seat like he's finished saying whatever it is he needs to and is waiting for me to comply. Not wanting to make this any weirder than it has to be, I do just that.

Silently, I shove my duffle bag back onto the bed and pad my way to the bathroom. My nerves triple as the door clicks shut behind me, serving as a reminder of what's to come. Soon, I will leave the comforting cocoon of Kade's room, only to be slapped in the face with the reality that is now my life. I hope I can survive it, or that Ryker will let me.

At least I'll have my dad.

The thought leaves me a tiny bit hopeful, while the rest of me dreads the impending turmoil that could possibly leave me stripped bare, scarred heart and all.

"If you need anything, just holler!" Kade zaps me out of my thoughts, and I flip on the water to acclimate the scalding temperature I crave.

"Thanks!" I call in return before stripping out of his shirt and welcoming myself into the perfect heat. A relaxed sigh bubbles to the surface as I let my worries melt away, even if it will only last a mere minute or two.

PAST
Our First Thanksgiving

Plucking a piece of freshly carved turkey off the decorative plate in the middle of my dining room table, I offer it to Brent, who's standing bare-chested a foot away. "Taste."

Dipping his head, eyes tilted upward, trained on my face, he takes a tentative nibble, grinning wickedly in my direction. A thrill races up my spine at that look. It's one I know well. One that says my man is up to no good. Silently, he steals the rest of the turkey from my fingertips. Then, he's on me. A big palm grabbing my ass makes me squeal as he propels us backward until my bottom hits the edge of the table. Not wasting a second, he effortlessly lifts me, placing my ass on the tabletop. My thighs spread open of their own accord, giving him space to step between. And he does.

Shoving down the top of my cotton dress, a tiny rumble of pleasure percolates in his throat as he exposes the peaks of my breasts. Grinning triumphantly, all teeth and devastating handsomeness, he drops the turkey there, and my insides catch fire, quivering with anticipation. He is up to no good, and it's glorious. Just like him.

I swallow hard.

"Turkey breast on my favorite breasts ... there's never been a better Thanksgiving," he groans, bending forward to clean the food off before I can formulate a single thought past the shock that's stunned me to near silence—aside from the moan that erupts when he drags the cups of my bra lower, baring my pert nipples.

Blowing there, he flicks his tongue out, lashing one. I moan loudly, squeezing around his hips, drawing him closer to my core as I lean back onto my elbows, careful not to the crush the feast I've laid out. My dress ruches up on its own, pooling under my baby bump. Brent's denim trapped cock settles against my panties; the fabric already soaked for him. I never knew sex could be this good for anybody. It's all consuming, all the time.

Wordlessly, Brent reaches over my head, and there's a clank before his fingers draw back, coated in a thick, brown gravy. He smears it over both nipples, swirling around each bud, drawing a tiny groan from the depths of my soul.

Licking his plump lips, his hungry gaze scalds my flesh. "I'm gonna enjoy eating our Thanksgiving dinner off your body."

"You're gonna..." I'm breathless, chest sharply rising and falling.

My clit weeps from neglect, needing him to touch me. To make me come. To fill me completely. Anything. I'm at his mercy. He can do whatever he pleases as long as he doesn't stop. I want to tell him that, but don't. Our feelings are something we never discuss. Although, I'm pretty sure he knows how I feel about him. It's in my every touch, every kiss, every moan. I can't hide them, even if I want to.

Delicately laving the gravy off one nipple, then the next, he stops to look up at my face, an expression of adoration there. Jesus. I really do love this man. "Yes, my little Tiger. I'm gonna feast on your body. How many orgasms do you think I can give you today?"

There's a glimmer of cockiness in his eyes like he knows he'll make me come fast and hard. It won't take but a few touches. We both know this. It never does. What can I say? It's impossible for me to resist. Which is what got us into this mess in the first place. Why my belly is swollen with his child. Why my heart is no longer mine, but his. Only his. Now and forever.

Pressing kisses down one breast, through the deep valley between, then up the other, he takes his time tasting and teasing. Knowing damn well what this does to me. What it always does. He's driving me mad.

The quivering of anticipation takes over until I'm a puddle of pliant, horny need. He continues to lick and suck my nipples, one and then the next, tugging them between his teeth before giving me a moment's reprieve. I beg him to go lower, and he does, ever so slowly dragging my dress down, peppering kisses along the way.

Exposing my bump, he delivers a lingering kiss there. It's sweet and tender. A lump forms in my throat at the sight. "Hello, my baby. I'm so happy you're in there. Daddy's excited to meet you." His lips skim lower, until he's kneeling, mouth mere inches from my panties. "Take cover in there. Daddy doesn't wanna poke ya in the head when he fucks Mommy on this table," he whispers.

Bracing myself on one arm, I slap the top of his skull hard enough that it echoes off the walls. "Your dick isn't *that* big," I tease.

It's true. He could be a foot long, and our child would still be fine. But ... okay ... he *is* huge. Like a good nine inches, and so thick, it hurts to spread my lips around it whenever he tries to fuck my mouth. I'd call it a monster cock, but that would inflate his ego even bigger. Which we don't need. He's got an ego large enough to fill the entire state of Indiana.

Another kiss is pressed to the underside of my belly as his hands clamp on my thighs, draping them over his wide shoulders. "You're killin' me, my little Tiger. Gonna give my dick an inferiority complex."

A giggle catches fire in my chest, and my eyes roll at the ridiculousness. Amused, my lips tip into a slight grin. "You're so full of it, Brent."

Shrugging his shoulders, my legs lift and fall with the movement. His mouth settles closer, a moist heat wafting over my cotton covered core. He mocks a hurt groan. "Now you're laughin' at my dick. That's not right, babes. Not right at all. You don't wanna make me cry, do ya?"

Knowing he's not serious, even if his tone suggests that he is, I sit up and shove his face into my aching pussy. A genuine groan vibrates there as he pokes his tongue out to taste me, circling my clit over the fabric. My head lulls back at the intense pleasure. "Yes," I hiss through clenched teeth.

Brent's mouth sucks over the cotton, soaking it in its entirety before he pulls away, heaving for air. I can't believe he's just as turned on by this as I am. God. I'm never gonna get enough of him. Ever. "Pass me the cranberry sauce," he commands, sounding like he's swallowed a cup of gravel.

Eager to see what he has up his sleeve, I do what he asks and offer him the bowl of homemade cranberry sauce with shaky hands. It's not as thick as the canned kind. It's better. He places his palm up for me to set it in, so I do. The quietness of the room, aside from our breathing, sparks goosebumps over my frame as I listen intently to the bowl *clanking* on the hardwood floor when it's set there. My insides somersault excitedly at the thought of what he'll do next. I can't wait! He's always keeping me guessing. Last week, we had sex in the bathtub—me riding him, water lapping at our sides. At first, I didn't think I'd like it. Then, when he controlled me from the bottom, thrusting into my depths, I was a goner. Coming at least five times, I panted and mumbled, melting into a deliriously sated mess. Afterward, I clung to him as he carried my spent body from the tub, dried me off, and took me to bed. Where we cuddled for the rest of the night. It was romantic. Even if he didn't think so.

A finger hooks into my panties, pushing the soppy fabric to the side. Cool air mixing with the warmth of his mouth lingering inches away from my flesh, makes me squirm. I bite my lip.

"I'm gonna eat cranberry sauce off this pussy..." His tongue flicks the tip of my inflamed clit, and I wail a wanton cry, legs vibrating with desperation. "You're gonna come for me five times, Kat, and I'm not gonna stop 'til ya do. Only then will I reward ya with my cock. Do ya understand?" He's as calm as the most deadly storm.

I nod frantically to answer his question. Yes. Yes. I understand, and I can't wait.

"Tell me," he demands, scraping his scruff along the inside of my thigh. It burns in the most delicious of ways.

"I—I—" Damn it. My legs won't stop shaking. I'm a mess already. Even my pussy is dripping. Nipples desperate for more attention, my trembling hands lift to twirl them between my fingers. A shock wave of ecstasy flashes to my pussy. I moan, swiveling my hips, desperate for any attention. I need more before I die, or go crazy. God! Why won't he give it to me?!

There's a clink, then a sudden coolness is slathered over my clit, massaging it in but not enough to make me come. "I asked you a question, my little Tiger. Now, you will answer me or I will not fuck you today."

"I need you to fuck me," I whine, pinching my nipples into sharp points.

"Why do you need me to fuck you, babe?" He kisses my clit, and I lift my hips, searching for more. Backing off, he chuckles, swiping a finger through my folds—stopping just long enough to encircle my empty core. He toys with me there, and I groan in frustration. "You're gonna tell me." He moves lower, coating my asshole with my juices, getting it nice and wet. "I may even put a little toy in here."

Oh dear, god! Yes, please! His cock in my pussy and a toy in my ass. It's the best feeling ever! Being filled to the brim, coming so hard that it's an out of body experience. He's taught me well.

"Yes. I—I want that." My voice wavers.

The tip of his finger breaches my back door, and I whimper. "Then tell me what I need to hear."

Swallowing thickly, I wet my lips before replying as steadily as possible. "I need your cock because I love it so much."

"Why do you love it?" His tone deepens as he nuzzles his cheek to my inner thigh, tenderly delivering a kiss or two there.

"Because it's the best I've ever had," I blurt unashamed. It's true, without a doubt.

"It's the only one you've ever had."

"Yes," I rasp.

A quick kiss is dropped to my throbbing clit. Dear God. He's gonna make me come soon.

"The only one you'll ever fuckin' have."

"Yes," I groan, rolling my nipples until the pain sizzles through me.

"You'll carry all my babies. And only my babies."

My heart flutters madly at his words, but I don't speak. My fingers falter as a ball of happiness unfurls in my gut, mingling with the pleasure and feelings I've yet to tell him aloud. They're mine to keep and cherish, for now.

"We're gonna have three kids, Kat. Three. And I'm gonna make you come so much you'll never want another dick. Never want another man. I'm it for you. Tell me I'm it for you." Emotions I can't pinpoint soak like rich whiskey into his words.

"You're it for me," I murmur, knowing that I mean it with every ounce of my being.

"Good," he growls. Then everything turns fluid as his mouth attacks my clit, ravenously sucking it like he hasn't eaten in a week. A thick finger slips into my pussy, and that's all she wrote. My world flips upside down, mind blanks, and I become a slave to Brent's unholy onslaught.

This is the best Thanksgiving ever.

PRESENT

This is the worst Thanksgiving ever.

Following my shower, I quickly dress in a pair of black maternity leggings and one of my oversized

AC/DC t-shirts. Once covered, Kade and I head downstairs to get some food to quell the pain in my stomach. It works, but the experience that come along with the sandwich and chips is a different story. Club members and visitors alike stare at me like I'm carrying the bubonic plague or something. To say it's disconcerting is putting it mildly. While I sit on a metal stool at the oversized butcher's block in the middle of their industrial sized kitchen, people pop in and out to chat a little with Kade. They don't think I notice the looks they are casting my way. I'm sure many are curious since nobody knew about Ryker's and my quasi-relationship until it was announced by Bear. Just as nobody knew that Ghost had a daughter. I'm an intruder on their turf. One that didn't ask to be lied to by two of the men I've loved the most. And I surely didn't ask to be treated like dog shit you'd scrape off the bottom of your shoe. Honestly, I bet it has a lot to do with unknowns. They probably want to know why I'm here, and pregnant. I'd wonder the same thing if I were them. Like—*What does she want?* The thing is, I only want honesty. That's all I ever wanted. I don't want Ryker. That's for sure. And as for my dad ... that remains to be seen.

The one positive thing about this whole experience has been Kade. He's been attentive, caring, and has no qualms with giving his fellow club members hell for throwing me dirty looks. He's protective, and I love it. It makes me feel kind of special to have a big guy like him going to bat for me. Kade is the first to do that for me since my daddy. Thankfully, he didn't have to do it all that often, as I didn't attract much attention, and flew mostly under the radar. Today has been the exception. Unfortunately, I'm the star of the show.

After the quick bite, Kade asks if I want a tour of the clubhouse. I politely decline, and we head back to his room where we talk about next to nothing as we wait for dinner. Which finally comes around, bringing us to this point that has me standing here, at the edge of my emotional safety net.

Thirty plus leather-clad guests are milling about in the backyard. I had wondered how everyone was going to fit for dinner. Now I know—as I stand inside the back door of the house, bare toes resting atop the cold metal strip of the threshold. The green grass strewn with various folding tables stretches before me. Some with folding chairs tucked underneath, draped in turkey printed tablecloths. The others lined along one side are bursting with fragrant food. It reminds me of a potluck. Not that I've been to many of those.

Standing in wait, Kade waves me forward, a friendly smile gracing his lips. Huffing a sigh, I take the first tentative step onto the concrete stoop. It's warmer under my toes. For good measure, I scan my surroundings a few more times. My dad, Ghost, notices me and jerks his chin in greeting, then goes about filling giant red cups with beer from a keg on the opposite end of the yard, where a table is covered with a shit-ton of liquor. Bear is impossible to miss, he has to be the second biggest man here. Asshole being the first. And there's no mistaking that he's here, because everybody has been eyeing him and my dad at least a dozen times each. There's a tension floating through the air so thick it could be cut with a knife. If I wasn't concerned for my dad's safety, I wouldn't care about *it*, or the glares Ryker seems to be tossing in his direction. Part of me wants to slap him silly, while the other hopes my dad handles his own.

Another few steps in the right direction, I draw more attention to myself, choosing to ignore the outright stares and faint comments. They're not mean, at least. More like whispers of "What's she doin' here?" and "What was Bear thinkin'?" ... Shit like that.

Sidling up next to Kade, he tosses an arm over my shoulder and escorts me over toward the head of a long table. He pulls a chair out for me that's three from the head, where I assume Bear will sit. Knowing that I don't want to walk around and socialize, I take the seat. He drops into the chair at my right, leaving a single one open next to him.

Out comes his knife again, doing what it always does, tracing his tattoos. I'm pretty sure it's a nervous habit. Or perhaps it's out of boredom. I haven't quite figured it out yet. Thankfully, he never breaks the skin, so I don't think he's a psycho. "We sit according to rank," he explains.

I wait for him to give me further clarification, but when it never comes, I ask, "Who else will sit here?"

Using his knife, he points from spot to spot, naming spaces. For a short-lived moment, I get an ounce of relief as he goes down my side of the table and the name Ryker isn't announced. But it soon fades into a stomach ache when the spots across from me are reserved for him and his wife, Vanessa. *Shit*.

Antsy, I jiggle my foot, silently mulling over my streak of bad luck. At least my dad will be next to Kade. And that weirdo outside his bedroom earlier today named Creeper ... he's going to be seated to my left. As soft rock music flutters through the air, dulling some of the chit-chat, I tilt my head back, take a deep breath, and close my eyes. Taking a moment of solitude, I pretend that I'm not here and that this isn't the first step into hell itself.

My senses kick into high gear without my sight, and the smell of delicious food blending with a small bonfire at the corner of the property makes my mouth water. For a few precious seconds, I daydream about being here under different pretenses—where I'm happily in love, and with my daughters as they spend time with their uncle and grandfathers. Everyone is nice to me in this dream. They all want to be my friend, and, most importantly, they adore my girls. I can almost hear Roxie and Scarlett squealing in delight as they eat slices of pumpkin pie that are drowning under a mountain of canned whipped cream—a family favorite. I'm partial to pecan pie myself, but the whipped cream is always a given.

A sliver of contentment douses my otherwise frazzled soul and a few notches of tension ease from my shoulders. I can do this. I can handle all of it with Kade by my side. My protector. Not that I'll need him. I won't. I'll be cordial and will try to keep a tight lid on the snarky remarks that usually get me into trouble.

When I reopen my eyes, there are people piling food onto plates across the way. Kade, who's no longer seated next to me, is striding back with two plates full of food. He sets one in front of me and retakes his spot. More and more people find their seats, including Vanessa and Ryker. Occupying myself by twiddling my thumbs in my lap, my stomach does an uneasy tumble as I hear the asshole grumble under his breath. He's obviously not pleased that I'm here—any more than I am. Good. Maybe that'll keep him from talking or looking at me tonight. So far, he hasn't. I would know. I've always been able to feel his eyes searing into me no matter where we are. Call it a sixth sense, or a Brent sense. I don't care what it's called, but it's something I've had since we first met all those years ago.

Bear is the last to take his seat, and the crowd quiets as if it's a huge deal. I haven't touched my food, so I bow my head out of respect and stare at the pile of mixed sustenance in front of me. It's a good thing I don't have that form of OCD where my foods can't touch, or I'd be even more miserable. Kade isn't a clean plate filler. Not that I'm complaining. At least I didn't have to get up.

Bear roughly clears his throat, capturing the group's attention. "As tradition, we're gonna go 'round the table and say what we're thankful for before we eat. I'll start first." There's a pause that feels like it takes ages before he speaks again. "I'm thankful for my club, my brothers, our family, and I'm especially thankful for Kat joinin' us here today." I dare to peek his way out of the corner of my eye.

Catching his gaze locked on me, he lifts a red cup into the air. "Here, here," he chants, and everyone follows suit by raising their glasses before my dad takes his turn.

"I'm thankful for my daughter, and granddaughters."

The sincerity in his words draws tears to my eyes. I blink them away. More *here, here's* are cheered, more alcohol consumed, then Kade is put on the spot. I can't believe I'm next. Since I'm not a member, can't they skip me? I hope they do.

"I'm thankful for..." Kade's arm drapes over the back of my chair, hot and comforting. I have to stop myself from leaning into it to dull the awkwardness of everyone's focus on me. He traces designs across the span of my shoulders with his fingertips, like he's trying to ease the tension. It helps, a little. "I'm thankful for family, an—"

"Care to remove your hand, brother?" Bre—Ryker growls lowly, cutting Kade off. The hairs on the back of my neck stand on end and I dip my head lower, praying that he stops talking. I don't want to hear that voice. I don't want to smell him. Look at him. Nothing. It's better this way.

Undeterred, Kade ignores his brother, his fingers drawing earnestly. I catch him out of my peripheral as he shoves a hand into his vest, right where he stows his knife. For three heartbeats, I wait for him to yank out the weapon to play. Another beat passes, and he surprises me by dropping his hand into his lap and squeezing his thigh so hard his knuckles turn to snow.

"I'm very thankful for family—" He grits his teeth, and Ryker curses loud enough for me to hear. "I'm thankful for *now* knowin' about my nieces and the charming Katrina."

On that note, Kade's hand cuffs around the back of my neck gently, clearly trying to get some point across. My belly shouldn't relish in the affection as much as it does. I can't tell you the last time I've been hugged by anyone other than my daughters. I kinda miss it.

Ryker doesn't like it one bit. A string of expletives thunders from his chest as I feel the table shake, and glance up just in time to see him shoot to his feet, chair collapsing onto the grass. Then, my father's on his feet, too. Fuming, Ryker shoots daggers from me to Kade, to my dad, and back again.

"Sit the fuck down, children," Bear bellows, leaning back in his chair, arms folded over that barrel chest. He's not amused by this in the least. And neither am I. This is stupid.

"I'm here to defend my daughter. I'm not sittin' down 'til he does." My dad jerks his head in Ryker's direction, eyes narrowing so sharply that the lines around them crinkle deeper, revealing his age. He's got one hand tucked into his vest.

Ryker snorts, rolling his blue eyes. "Right, because I'm gonna hurt Kat." Sarcasm drips like rich honey from his lips. "That's fuckin' ridiculous to hear comin' from you, *old man.*"

I'm not sure if that was supposed to be a taunt or not, but my dad isn't taking the bait as he remains planted, glaring, body taut. From here, I can make out an older tattoo on his forearm. It says daughter inside a white banner that's surrounded by some skulls and roses. It's kinda pretty, in a manly way. Below it are ... *holy shit*! He has my daughters' names tattooed on him, too! A fierce bolt of joy explodes inside me, and I can't help it when I crack the tiniest of smiles. Cupping my mouth with my hand, I hide the evidence of my happiness. I don't want people to take my reaction the wrong way, and think I'm enjoying this sad display of dominance.

When I was a kid, my dad didn't have any ink. Now, he's sleeved, and it's a cool surprise. It suits him. I always thought he was too much of a bad boy not to rock some ink. And since his hair is longer than before, curling just above his collar, the tattoos definitely fit him. He doesn't quite look like the man I knew growing up. But he's still my dad, and I'm still his female mini-me.

"You've already done enough, Ryker," Dad snips.

"*I ... see ...* Pot's callin' the kettle black." Ryker's biceps bulge as he crosses his arms over his beefy chest. I'd forgotten how sexy that actually looks.

Irritated by this pathetic pissing contest in my honor, I take a calming breath before I stand, drawing all eyes our way. As if they weren't already glued here to begin with. Kade, not letting me go at this alone, shoots up from his seat but remains quiet at my side. I siphon some of his inner strength, cup my belly with one hand, then summon my attitude to the surface. "Sit down, both of you, and be quiet." My scowl swaps from Dad to Ryker. "This is already weird enough without you acting like two baboons ready to fling shit at each other. So let's eat. Everyone's food is gettin' cold. And Dad..." Cautiously, he lowers into his chair, eyes keenly watching me. "I still love you, and we can talk afterward. Ignore the jerk, he's not worth either of our breaths."

Still standing, Ryker's face falls from its bravado just a smidge when I aim my disappointment in his direction. "Sit down." I point to him like a teacher scolding her student. As anticipated, he doesn't budge and his jaw clenches, nostrils flaring. Yes, he's a stubborn mule, just as I am. That's one of the many, many, reasons things could never have worked between the two of us. At least not now. I don't think I was as stubborn back then. Years of single mothering does that to ya. It's either that or be walked all over by two equally obstinate daughters, and that wasn't an option.

"He doesn't need to listen to you." Vanessa grows some balls, and I glance her way, ready to take on the world if this woman really wants to throw down. I have zero tolerance for bitchy, self-righteous, know-it-all chicks; especially when I'm trying to defuse a situation that involves me. Not her.

"Do you think it's acceptable to act this way on Thanksgiving?" I'm composed as I wait for her response, but it doesn't come. Tilting her head to the side, she flips her luxurious black hair over her shoulder in defiance. Great, and here I thought we could at least be cordial after all that's gone down. Looks like I've got myself another enemy in the making.

Keeping my eyes glued on her, and refusing to spare another glance at her husband, I speak from the heart, both hands rubbing my daughter. "Listen, I know this situation isn't ideal. You didn't know about me. Nobody did." I sweep my gaze down the tables and back, watching people nod along with my confession. "You can be pissed all ya want. Defiant. Juvenile. I don't care. I'm too old to deal with all that. Do Ryker and I have history? Yeah, we do. I'm the mother of two of his children. That's the facts whether anyone likes it or not." Kade rests a hand on my shoulder in support, as if he knows how hard this is for me. I welcome the boost of strength. "I'm thankful for being alive. Thankful that my father's alive. That I have two beautiful daughters I've raised on my own, with only the help of my mother. Who, when I was growing up, wasn't really a mother at all. I'm not gonna fight with anybody here. Maybe, for once, you and everybody else should stop going on the defensive and think about what I'm going through. What Kade's going through..." I pat his hand reassuringly. "I had no clue Ryker, who *I* knew as Brent, was in a motorcycle club. Let alone, that my father wasn't really dead. Have you lost anyone, Vanessa?"

Emotionless, she shakes her head, slouching in her chair, huffing childishly. Last night, beneath the dim lights of the house, her age was hard to tell. But now, in the sinking daylight, I can see her tanned, unblemished skin and the lack of age lines on her face. Not even a crinkle at her eye, or a line across her forehead. If I had to guess, she couldn't be any more than twenty-four. Probably younger. I've never understood a man's need to date women significantly younger than them. I get that they make one feel youthful and that their bodies which have endured less are enjoyable. There's nothing wrong with that. On the same token, there is nothing wrong with bodies like mine, either. Women are beautiful regardless of age, the size of our waists, or wrinkles. It irks me when some men don't see our value. I know that I am not that old. I just feel that way all the time. My mom says there's an eighty-year-old woman trapped inside me. Apparently, I view life differently than others my age.

Disappointed by Vanessa's reaction, or lack thereof, I keep on. "Well, I have. First, my mother when I was a child. Second, my dad when I was fourteen. Third ... well, that doesn't matter anymore. The point is: I'm not here to fuck with anyone's life. I'm here to find some of the shattered parts of mine. As hopeless as that sounds, that's all I've ever wanted; to feel whole again. And if you've ever been so broken that you didn't know what jagged edge fits where, then you'd get what I'm sayin'. If not, consider yourself blessed for not havin' to go through some of the shit that me and plenty others have." Having calmly said my peace, I retake my seat and look to Bear to make sure he's not pissed at me for creating an even bigger scene.

Inclining his head in my direction, he smirks. "Fuck tradition. Like Kat said, our food's gettin' cold. I think I can speak for everybody when I say we're thankful for our families." Bear raises his cup, and I lift mine that's filled with ice water. "Here, here," we cheer and dig in.

Stuffing our faces serves as the perfect distraction. The turkey is juicy, the mac-n-cheese extra cheesy with that perfect crust on the top, the green bean casserole is by far the best I've tasted, and these chocolate chip cookies are to die for. For once, I'm thrilled to see the cranberry sauce didn't make it onto my plate. I haven't been able to eat that stuff since Brent disappeared, and that has everything to do with a little Thanksgiving fuck session we had when I was pregnant with Roxie. Unfortunately, that's a memory I'll never be able to scrub from my brain. Trust me, I've tried.

Kade carts my empty plate to the trash and refills my water. As the sun dips below the horizon, the men and women get up from the table to consume mass quantities of alcohol and socialize. The sunset showcasing an array of bright oranges and the tiniest kiss of blood red is gorgeous.

Standing behind my chair, Kade drops his palms to my shoulders, kneading them with the perfect pressure. Groaning in pleasure, I let my eyes drift closed. Damn. That feels amazing.

"Good?" There's a tickled inflection in Kade's voice.

"Soooo good," I purr.

He chuckles. "You're doin' real good, Kat."

"So are you with those magical fingers." I roll my shoulders, and he digs in deeper, eliciting a carnivorous moan from my belly.

His digits halt mid-squeeze, and Kade roughly clears his throat. Why's he stopping? Did I say something wrong? "Erm … D-do ya care to head over to the bonfire? We've got chairs set up over there. Or we can go back to my room if you're done for the night. Whatever ya want." The massage resumes, more tentative than before, as if he's not sure if he should be touching me any longer.

To decompress the sudden change in mood, I ask, "Are Ryker or Vanessa over there?" They left their seat seconds after they finished shoveling food into their pie holes. I tried not to notice Vanessa grabbing Ryker's forearm and steering him to wherever she wanted. It seemed a little bitchy to me. But that's not any of my concern.

"No. The coast is clear. I'm pretty sure my dear sister-in-law is kickin' his ass by now."

The prickle of annoyance stiffens my frame, and I frown. I don't know why that bugs me as much as it does. It shouldn't. I hate Ryker.

Checking my stupid emotions, I change the subject. "So tell me more about yourself, Kade."

I sense him shrug. "Not much to tell."

"Now that can't be true."

"It is."

"No kids? Wife? Girlfriend? Job?"

Skilled thumbs work gingerly into the base of my neck. It's utterly divine. "Not yet, nope, nope, and I was what you'd call an E.R. nurse before I started workin' full time for the club."

"Doin' what exactly?" That's pretty crappy that he's no longer a nurse. However, it makes sense as to why he's so good at the medical stuff. Something tells me he takes pride in caring for people. Me being case and point.

"Can't say." He taps my shoulder, and I pry my eyes open. "Hey. Look over there." Pointing toward the edge of the property, next to a large tree, is a group of scantily-clad women gossiping amongst themselves. I didn't see them at dinner. "Those are what we call club whores. You probably saw some of 'em here last night."

"So that's who slobs on your knob?" I snicker, witnessing a chick adjust her heaving bosom. If the curvy brunette pushes them any higher, she's gonna suffocate herself. And here I thought my jugs were bigger than Annette's. Not that that's her name.

Kade rewards me with one of his deep, belly laughs. It's the kind that you know he feels throughout his entire body. "Wh-who in the fuck says that kinda shit?" His amusement slowly tapers off, still holding its edge.

"I do?" What can I say? After spending a day with the man, I'm already at ease around him. What's not to like?

"You're nuts," he chortles. "But yeah, they're who I fuck whenever I need to get my dick wet."

"Which one's Janet?" I nod in their direction, remembering Creeper had mentioned her name.

Kade's deft fingers slip into the base of my scalp, and it feels so damn good, he could just about lull me to sleep. My eyes flutter shut of their own accord. Sweet Jesus. He's a magician. Hopefully, he's in the market for a new best friend. I'd like to apply for the job if that means I get moan worthy massages out of it.

"She's the blonde."

I peek for a second, noticing a curvy towhead with thick thighs and tattoos cascading down both arms, staring in our direction. "Looks like someone wants a piece of that dick now."

"I'm busy. She can wait." He's fierce.

"You sure? 'Cause I should probably mingle a bit. I'm sure your dad wants to have a few words. And I am leaving tomorrow."

"You do what ya want. They can all wait until you're ready. They're the assholes who started this shit. You don't have to work on anybody's time other than your own."

That's another thing I'm coming to adore about Kade. He's not only blunt, but he also cares about my feelings. More so than anyone else.

"Thanks. But I think you need to, as you say, get your dick wet." Reluctantly moving away from his masterful hands, I use the edge of the table to help me push up from the chair. Turning to face him, I reach out to pat him on his hard-as-a-rock pec, smiling graciously. "Don't worry about me."

Laying his hand over mine, flattening my palm to his chest, his heart pulses strong and steady, just like the man it belongs to. Tilting my head back so that I can see his face, our gazes lock. "You're my family, Kat. I'm gonna worry about you. And I'm not about to go fuck some hole and leave ya to fend for yourself."

"How about a quick blow job, then?" I grin cheekily.

"If you insist." There's a twinkle of mirth in his eye as he bends down to place a single kiss upon my upturned forehead. The warmth of his surprisingly soft lips seeps into my veins, filling me with a sense of peace I didn't know I was missing.

"I do. Very much," I whisper, not wanting to ruin the oddly tender moment. "It's the least you deserve for taking care of me."

Nodding, a small smile gracing his lips, Kade tucks my arm through his and escorts me to the bonfire. The cooling grass squishes through my toes, sending shivers up my legs. He deposits me into a folding chair, kissing my forehead once more. "See ya later, beautiful. I won't be far. Just over there," he says, indicating where that blonde woman is waiting for him, her feet shifting excitedly. Somebody is quite smitten with the handsome Kade. Not that I blame her. He seems like quite the catch. Too bad I'd fallen in love with the wrong brother. *Gah.*

Teasingly, I pinch his side, finding a thin layer of skin stretched over muscle, which takes away half of the pinching fun. "Go get your jiggy on," I sing-song, and he winks at me before sauntering over to the foxy lady who's about to rock his world. Judging by the wild and crazy tongue action they jump straight into, I'm certain he's gonna have a blast. His hand already gripping a juicy portion of ass.

I miss being groped like that.

Disregarding the longing ache in my chest, I turn my sights toward the blazing fire. The ache's not there because Janet is getting some hot Kade action. No. As much as I find him attractive, it's not in a sexual, I-wanna-jump-his-bones way. Mostly, I'm green with envy because of the attention. I remember that feeling of overwhelming lust that steals all logic and turns you into a horny ball of need every time that special person breathes in your direction. Hell. If they even breathe within the same ten square miles. I used to feel that way once upon a time when young love was a thing. That was before I understood what heartbreak and bitterness felt like. Now I've got that in spades. That shit is like super glue. It just won't let go, no matter how many times you visit the psychologist or try to drown your sorrows in the bottom of a wine bottle.

"Hey." The distinct voice of my father rips me from my dark musings, and I glance over my shoulder as he sets a paper plate piled with whipped cream into my lap. A plastic fork is tucked into the side, keeping the handle from getting messy. "I snagged ya some pecan pie," he explains, dropping a napkin on the arm of my chair before taking the seat to my right, and scooting it closer.

Ogling the creamy mountain in mouthwatering awe, I lick my lips nice and slow. "I—I can't believe you remembered." Emotions clog my throat.

"I remember everythin' about ya, Peanut." There's a raw benevolence in his voice that plucks at my frozen heartstrings. The thick ice cracks into a spider web pattern but doesn't break. *Shoo*. That was a close one.

Peanut. It's been so long since anyone has used that nickname. And God knows, I've had many nicknames in my life; Kat being the most prevalent.

Swallowing nervously, I bite the corner of my lip, uncertain of what I'm supposed to say. What *do* you say? Many times I dreamed of what I could tell him. Now here I am, tongue-tied, on the verge of an internal meltdown as my heart uses my ribs as a punching bag. Hot damn, this is so fucking surreal. He's really here. Right next to me. Giving me pecan pie. Observing my every move. We'd eaten dinner feet apart, but nothing felt more real than this does right this second, where I can reach out and touch him. Touch. My. Dad! I ... fuck ... I'm not sure how I'm supposed to take this.

Moisture gathers at the corners of my eyes.

"Don't sweat it, Peanut. Just eat your pie, then we'll talk whenever you're ready."

Numbly, I nod my compliance and dig into the sugary bliss. Minutes slip by as I swirl my fork in the whipped cream and carve out bite after bite of the homemade pie. It's more delicious than I remember. The noise of people conversing, faint moans, and the fire crackling are drowned out by the thumping in my ears as blood surges through my veins. My hand shakes when I take another taste and slowly churn the yumminess in my mouth to bide some time. I still can't believe he's here.

Finished way too soon, I rest the plate on my lap, attention focused on the glowing embers at the bottom of the pit. The heat wafting off kisses my cheeks in a pleasant way. Where are the marshmallows when ya need them? Or do bikers not roast marshmallows? My daughters' sure love charring them over the small fire pit in our backyard.

Shit, I've got to stop wasting time. It's now or never. Tomorrow is going to come way too soon.

A knot lodges in my throat as I open my mouth to speak. "I ... I saw you have Roxie and Scarlett's names tattooed on your forearm." That's as good of an opening remark as he's going to get. Why is this so damn hard? He's my dad. It shouldn't be this difficult. Should it?

"We've all got 'em."

Now that captures my attention enough that I angle myself so I can see him head on. "What does that mean?"

Dad traces the girls' names on his arm with his fingertip. The letter S is tattooed on his knuckle, and on the one beside it is a fancy O. I wonder what it spells out. "Bear and I went and got their names tattooed on us 'bout five years ago."

"Why in the hell would you do that?" My voice jumps a few octaves, reminding me too much of my mother. I shiver at the thought.

Daddy shrugs, and pushes his tattooed fingers through his hair, discharging a pent-up sigh. "I dunno, Peanut. Why do ya think? You're my daughter, and they're my grandbabies. Whether or not you think so, Bear and I do care about you and the girls. His tat's on his back so Kade couldn't see it. But it's got your name there, too, inside this heart with roses surroundin' it."

"Like the roses in the Sacred Sinners emblem?"

"Yup."

This is so fucking strange. My insides concur as this bizarre sensation bangs around in my chest like a damn game of pinball. Out of the corner of my eye, I notice Bear standing by himself a few yards away, gazing impassively in our direction, a beer clutched in his big paw. If the shifter stories I read were nonfiction, he'd be an alpha werebear with silver fur, tender blue eyes, and a jowl that'd make the biggest brawlers run for cover. Jeez, that's just ridiculous. My brain needs to shut the hell up. Shaking my head to rid it of outrageous thoughts, I then lift my hand to wave him over. For a second, a flash of hesitation washes over his features before he nods once, grabs a nearby chair, sets it next to my dad, and drops into it, expelling a leaded groan.

Dad sideways glances at Bear. "I was tellin' her about our tattoos."

Casually, Bear sips on his beer. "Which one?"

"The names," Dad replies.

A redness tinges Bear's cheeks as he swings his attention to the fire.

Knowing he's uncomfortable with the topic, I move to something less blush-worthy. Although I gotta say, a big man with crimson cheeks is kinda adorable. I press my lips together to smother a grin. "I gotta be honest with ya. This is still weird for me. I'm not sure what I'm supposed to ask. Like ... is it okay if I ask if I have any other brothers and sisters? Or if you've remarried? I mean, I know after Mom and you divorced, you didn't date anyone ... I ... I dunno ... I guess I wanna know everything? Or whatever you can tell me."

Dad's tentative hand reaches across the space between us and hovers above my forearm that's relaxing on the armrest. He waits there, suspended for what feels like hours until I give him a reassuring nod. He exhales gratefully, tension melting from his shoulders and face as his clammy palm rests atop my arm. Another crack in the foundation of my frozen heartstrings splinters outward.

The bulk of Dad's Adam's apple bobs in his throat as he audibly gulps. "I don't have any other kids, and I've never remarried. But I do have a partner." Dad's other hand reaches out for Bear and pats him on the knee. Flinching at the touch, nostrils flaring, Bear fists and unfists his hands in his lap, once, twice, before he pats my dad's hand in return.

What ... the? Wait ... What? I ... Uh ... Seriously? He's...

There's an exchange of something profound from Dad's eyes to Bear's when they lock gazes with one another. It's a look that says Bear isn't pleased. Though, by the tiny incline of his head and the dip in his eyes, he's still yielding to whatever it is they're communicating through unspoken words. Then, their touch is gone as fast as it came. Bear's sight drops back to the fire, where he tucks his arms across his broad chest, slouching in his chair, beer cup nestled between those thick thighs.

Dad clears his throat. "Bear and I are..." Tapering off, a silence stretches.

"You're what?" The twinge in my gut tells me all I need to know, but I have to hear it from him first.

"We're..." He hesitates.

"We're together," Bear snarls under his breath.

One second, Dad is seated, hand on my arm, shifting nervously. The next, he's out of his chair and punching Bear straight in the chest. Bear's chair snaps back from the mighty blow, taking him down with it. The noise echoes in the yard. Scrambling to his feet, he glares at Dad before charging him like a beast, knocking him to the ground and straddling his stomach. Dad swings his fist, connecting solidly with his jaw. Bear's head snaps to the side, blood spewing from his lips just like you'd see in a fighter movie.

"I was supposed to tell her, you fuckin' asshole!" Dad yells.

A blood-stained grin that's part demonic, part loving, is cast my father's way at the same instant he strikes Bear again. Except, this time, he misses when Bear catches his fist, immediately pinning it above his head in the grass. The other soon joins it, rendering him helpless. Adrenaline flowing, I wait a second to be upset, or have this need to defend my family, but when it doesn't come, I sit back, rub my belly, and watch the most entertaining thing I've seen all day unfold.

Boys will be boys.

Chest heaving, eyes manic, Dad digs his boot heels into the turf and thrusts his hips off the ground, trying to dislodge the brute seated on top of him. Bear doesn't budge and chuckles instead. A small crowd gathers, looking more amused than concerned. Kade slides up next to me, his hand relaxing on my shoulder in silent support. He seems to do that a lot.

"We've been over this plenty of times, you feisty motherfucker." Bear bends over far enough that he head-butts Dad. It's not done in malice. It's friendlier than that. Sweet, almost. If pinning your man to the ground, after he tried to kick your ass, is sweet. Maybe it is for them. "You're not allowed to punch me unless we're in the bedroom." Bear growls like ... well ... a bear, the top of his thick beard brushing over Dad's pursed lips, a deep crease formed between his brows.

"This isn't foreplay, dickhead. This is serious!" Dad is furious, jerking underneath the man's weight but knowing damn well that's not going to do him any good. Bear has to be at least twice his size.

Grouchy, Bear shakes his head. "I told ya I didn't want her to know 'til I knew if she liked me! But, nooo ... you didn't listen, did ya? If it weren't for me, she wouldn't even be here! So stop you're damn strugglin'. You and I both know that I could fuck your mouth right now, and there's not a damn thing you could do to stop me. So stop wigglin'. You're givin' me a hard-on, motherfucker!"

Oh. My. God. This is the funniest thing I've ever seen in my entire life. Bear's angry at Dad for getting him sexually aroused, and he's concerned I wouldn't like him. That's endearing as hell, isn't it? I mean, big, bad, Bear, with all those wild tattoos, prez of a club, and he's worried about me liking him? I don't know many bikers, but if you told me they cared this much, I wouldn't have believed ya.

Covering my mouth with my hand, I giggle behind my fingers, smiling.

In the dimness of the firelight that's casting shadows over his face, I catch the exaggerated roll of

Dad's eyes. "You worry too much about everything." His tone is composed. "She's my daughter. I love her very much. And I love you, too, ya big fuckin' softie. Of course, she's gonna love you. You're bein' paranoid. Like always."

"She didn't know you were gay," Bear declares.

"She does now. Since you fuckin' told her."

Kade kneels on one knee, whispering into my ear. "Creeper said they've been arguin' about this all day."

My breath catches for a beat.

"About tellin' me?"

His hot breath fans across my cheek, sending a fresh batch of gooseflesh down my frame. "It doesn't bother ya, does it?"

"That my dad is gay?" I mutter.

"Yeah."

It's sad that in this day and age people have to ask anybody that. I work with a lesbian couple, and my new neighbor, the one who bought the house that Brent lived in, is gay. And I'm talking drag queen, teach-me-how-to-do-makeup, put-me-to-shame-in-beauty gay. One of these days, whenever I snatch up the courage, I'm going to ask Anthony to teach me how to wear makeup like he does. It's gorgeous, and not so over the top, you wince. He bought the place two years ago, and he's the best neighbor I've ever had. Plus, the girls love the crap out of him. Mainly because every time he decides he doesn't like one of his sparkly outfits, he donates it to my daughters, who love playing dress up. That might sound weird to some people. Nonetheless, we love Anthony and bake him cookies for his birthday and Christmas every year.

So no; I don't really care if my dad is gay. I care more about the fact that he's not been in my life. That he had to fake his death. That he didn't come for me. There's just too many variables that matter more than someone loving someone of the same sex. Maybe I'm too flippant about all this. Or the more obvious choice is that I still feel like this is a dream I'll eventually wake up from. I can't decide which. Most people would probably be freaking the hell out. I probably should be, too. But I'm not. Life is too short to get angry about someone's sexual preference. My father or not. It makes no difference. He's alive. That's what I'm choosing to focus on. Not the sting of betrayal that lingers under the surface for losing all these years together.

Turning the tables on Kade, I test, "Do *you* care that your dad is gay?"

"He's not gay. And no," he explains.

"What?!" I whisper-scream, frowning, as I watch my dad and Bear get off the ground to retake their seats.

"He's bisexual and has been since I was a kid. Let them tell you all about it. I just came by to make sure everything was okay." He kisses my cheek and saunters off before I can get another word in edgewise.

"Sorry about that." Bear is the first to speak. "I'm not usually that careless with words."

"Yes, he is," Dad adds with a pleased smile. "The club, he runs with an iron fist. But when it comes to family, he's a big fuckin' teddy bear."

Wiping his blood encrusted lips with the back of his hand, Bear grumbles his disagreement, adding a few choice cuss words into the mix.

"Soooo." I toss my paper plate and fork into the flames and settle in for a long night of talking. There's a lot I need to know.

Kade returns to our group momentarily to hand his Prez and VP two red cups of beer. They give their thanks, and he disappears again to perv on that tatted blonde.

Without hesitation, Dad cuts to the meat of the story. "I'm gay. Always been gay." He holds his palm up. "And before ya ask why I married your mother and had you, listen to what I've got to say."

Nodding, I wave him onward.

"I met your mom in high school, which you already know. We were friends. I was closeted, but knew I was battin' for the same team, and she knew it, too. That's why we got married. So both of our parents would get off our backs about settling down. We wanted a kid. Thank fuck it only took a handful of tries to get her knocked up. As I'm sure she told ya, I was into sellin' drugs. She didn't like it. Hell. I knew it was wrong, but it was bringin' in the cash, so I didn't wanna stop. That's why she divorced me. She didn't wanna get caught up in the drugs and go to jail if I ever got in trouble and they put her away for knowin' about it. I didn't blame her for that. And

111

yeah, I loved her in my own way. Even felt betrayed she left me..."

"She left both of us," I interject, recalling the devastation we both felt when she cut ties. My dad still loved her after their divorce. I thought he refused to date other women because of that. I guess not.

My grams has always been a traditional kinda woman. You get married and have babies right out of high school. Your husband takes care of you, and you're a homemaker—cooking and cleaning for your family. Always having dinner on the table at six sharp. Starching and ironing your husband's clothes, and never raising your voice in anger. Crap like that. It doesn't surprise me that she put pressure on my dad. She did the same to my uncle and look where that ended up—him in a loveless marriage with a hag for a wife. I cannot stand my aunt or her offspring that are my cousins, who I refuse to claim as family. They're all spoiled brats.

Though, for my mom, I suppose she married my dad because she grew up dirt poor. My grandma was a real piece of work, or so I've been told. She was a man-eater. Dating lots of married men—truck drivers mostly. She's been gone now for quite some time. My mother had cut her out of our lives before she ran off to Vegas. I guess the apple doesn't fall too far from the tree—like mother, like daughter ... both man-eaters. It's just sad that my parents couldn't marry for love and did it out of convenience. That kinda sucks for me, too. I'm the product of a business transaction. Luckily, I broke that cycle, because my daughters were born out of all-consuming, make-your-heart-sing love. From my side of things, at least. I can't speak for Asshole's. And, frankly, his opinion doesn't count.

"I didn't know she'd do that. But I couldn't change it. I kept you, so that's all that mattered. She wanted outta that life. So she moved to Vegas. That was her deal. Not mine," Dad says, seeming to settle more into the conversation, body lounging comfortably in his chair.

"Okay. So we know all about the mom stuff. She left. I hated her ... blah ... blah ... blah..." I cut my hand through the air to skip those other painful parts, headed straight to the finale. "Then you died." Even as I attempt to keep it under wraps, my emotions get the best of me. A sob curdles in my throat, choking my words. Dad's face crumples and moisture gathers in his eyes, shining in the firelight. He wipes them away with the back of his hand, and Bear, who I didn't think was paying attention, leans closer to squeeze my Dad's shoulder.

Morosely, he bobs his head, lips tipped into a severe frown. "I died. Big Dick, the national prez, helped make that happen. I'm sure Bear told ya I can't say much. 'Cause I can't. But what I can tell ya is that I got into some shit with some bad men. They threatened to take ya. So I went to the club and begged them to help me, help you..."

A stagnate pause has my heart beating faster, waiting for him to finish his story. Only it doesn't come. His hands fumble in his lap instead, like he's unsure of what to say next.

"And the rest is history?" I remark to circumvent the impending awkwardness.

Dad shrugs. It's a sad, defeated one that makes me want to reach out and wrap him in my arms. "More or less, yeah. I'm sorry I can't tell ya more ... That I did this shit to ya ... That I ... *fucked up your life.*"

Those welling tears in his eyes drip down his cheeks, and he loses it, outright sobbing. Suddenly, a rush of emotion overtakes me, and I join in. A shattered wail of pain rips from my soul as wetness streams down my cheeks. I clutch my chest, bending forward as the culmination of all these years without him bear down on my heart. It hurts so badly. My vision blurs, glasses fog, and I bite my lip to keep from screaming as the pain of my past, that I locked up tight, tears open, leaving my raw insides to bleed out. I try to be strong, but it's impossible. Hiccupping a hoarse cry, I crumble, losing myself, weeping through the shudders that wreak havoc over my body. A large form plucks me from the chair with ease and places me onto a set of strong legs. Curling my knees up, I burrow into the heat. The scent of leather, spicy musk, and sadness embraces my senses as arms hook around my body, hugging me so tightly that I fear I might break.

"I'm so sorry, Peanut," my dad chokes, his body trembling in succession with mine. "I'm so, so, so, sorry. I love you so damn much."

Draping my arms around his neck, stuffing my face against his collarbone, tears soaking into his shirt, I hang on for dear life, allowing myself to finally let go. To weep for the lost years, and the moments stolen from us. For my children not having a grandpa. I sob for myself and the little girl who was scarred by the loss of her father. I cry for my dad. For what could have been. Buckets of tears rain down as my heart gallops in my chest, my forehead sweating, soul bared, ready to dump this heavy burden into the waiting abyss.

It feels like hours as we hug each other, never wanting to let go or say goodbye. By the time the waterworks drip their very last drop, and I can finally take my first deep breath again—my guts feel mangled, face sticky with snot, and my eyes nearly swollen shut. Filling my lungs is cathartic, like I'm breathing in a new life. A new beginning. Kicking the fallen limbs of agony away from the base of my internal tree, I allow fresh limbs to grow anew. A sense of marrow-deep contentment seeps throughout me, making itself right at home.

For a few beautiful, unadulterated moments, we just breathe together, father and daughter. Until a buzzing heat sears into my flesh, bringing my head up from its daddy cocoon. It's the warmth I feel when a specific someone is watching me. It's Ryker. I know it. I can't see him, but I can sense his presence. It fucks with my equilibrium, so I shake my head, clean my messy glasses off using my shirt, then snuggle back into my daddy's lap, trying to ignore that itchy sensation. When I was younger, I used to relish in the fact that I knew when his eyes were on me. Now, it's like a yeast infection that won't go away.

A kiss is dropped into my damp hair. "I love you, Peanut. Please forgive me."

Bottom lip wobbling, nose nuzzling against the wet cotton of his t-shirt, I reply a shaky, "I—I love you, too, Dad. And I forgive you." Desperately, I hug him a little tighter. "I'm just happy you're alive. And … it doesn't matter to me if you like to be fucked in the ass. I like it, too. There's nothing wrong with that."

Bear barks a throaty laugh beside us, and I want to slap myself in the face for saying one of the stupidest things aloud, once again. A humored rumble knocks around in my dad's chest but doesn't quite make it out of his mouth. "I don't like to be fucked in the ass." He gives me a squeeze. "But I'm happy to hear that you're okay with it if I did."

Well, I guess that answers the unspoken question. Which is none of my business. My father, the top. I would've never guessed that when looking at him and Bear. Wowza. That's … okay … my thoughts are definitely not allowed to go there. We're Switzerland, here. No toppy, bottom, gay thoughts permitted. *Scrub, scrub, scrub.* Erasing them from my vocabulary now. You should scrub yours, too, because I know what you're thinkin'.

That flushed heat burns into the back of my neck, standing the hairs on end. To distract myself, I decide to ask more questions in the safety of my dad's embrace. "How'd you and Bear get together?"

"I'd been here about four years. Already patched as VP when I came out."

"They didn't know you were gay?"

"Nope."

"Did they care?"

"Some of 'em did. This isn't the most acceptin' kinda club to be in. But Bear set 'em straight. Told 'em if they had a problem with me, they'd have to go through him. That he'd beat 'em first, then dump their bodies in a fuckin' ditch to bleed to death."

I gasp. "He actually said that?"

"Sure did. At a fuckin' party, no less. Two guys walked away. Didn't wanna be in a club with no fag. Even though they never gave two fucks that Bear's been openly bisexual since they'd met him. Guess me not likin' tits was the deal breaker. So Bear tracked 'em down, roughed 'em up, burned their colors, and told 'em they better never set foot 'round here again, or he'd put a bullet between their eyes."

"Are you sure we're talking about the same Bear?"

I have a hard time picturing that big man acting like a violent badass. Sure, he's scary and intimidating in his own way. Yet, in another, he looks so damn cuddly all ya wanna do is snuggle into his warmth. I bet that's what my dad does. A gooey sensation unfolds in my belly at the thought. My dad is happy here. And that's all I can really hope for. This is his true home.

Dad snorts his amusement. "Yeah, we're talkin' about the same Bear. He's ruthless if you're disrespectful. I woulda helped him fuck those men up, too. If he would have let me. But, he was worried about us gettin' caught. And with me bein' dead and all, that doesn't look too good to the police."

"Makes sense." I nod into his chest, loving the smell and committing it to memory, so when I have to leave tomorrow, I can remember it for always.

"He doesn't wanna admit this to ya, but I seduced him. So don't go thinkin' he was tryin' to get with me or somethin'," Bear comments gruffly.

Dad chuckles. "I'm tryin' *not* to scar my daughter here, Bear. Don't be layin' it on thick. All you need to know, Peanut, is that we're together. And that, for the most part, the members don't care. Gay, bi, or otherwise, we're still the same men. I hope you're okay with that."

Bear pipes up. "No. That ain't all she needs to know. She needs to know that your club prez was naked in your bedroom—"

"Shut the hell up, Bear," Dad growls, chest vibrating viciously at the seriousness of his words.

"...on his goddamn hands and knees, askin' you to fuck me. That you told me no. But I ordered ya to..."

"I said, enough!"

Pressing my lips to his shirt, I curb a giggle.

I can't believe I'm hearing this.

"...and ya still told me to fuck off. So I forced myself on you. And ya still fought me the entire motherfuckin' time. He's a stubborn bastard, darlin'. He wouldn't have me for two years. Two. *Damn.* Years. He said we were *too* good of friends." Glee dances in Bear's tone, complementing that edge of adoring frustration.

Dad huffs in exasperation, his hand rubbing my side. "I can't believe you fuckin' told her that, you dumbass."

I grin at their cute banter. It's either that or truly wrap my head around all he's confessed. My. Dad. Is.

Gay. Not that I have a problem with that. But that's a lot to take in, ya know? Just like everything else.

"What? People talk 'round here. I didn't want her to know, yet. But since you went and told her, I'm gonna tell her the rest. You can't give half a story, Ghost."

"It's not half a fuckin' story. She's not one of the brothers we're talkin' to. It's me *not* tellin' my daughter how you basically raped me the first time we ever had sex." He's getting pissed. I know that quiet rage that lingers under the surface. He used that on me once, when I'd snuck out to kiss a boy when I was twelve. Needless to say, the kid never talked to me again, and I was grounded for a month. It sucked.

"I knew what I wanted. So I took it. And I didn't see your dick complainin'," Bear snips.

Woo ... Okay ... Yeah ... we've hit that TMI brick wall. It's one thing to be open-minded. It's another to hear about your dad's erection. Yuck! Knowing he gets them is one thing. Hearing about it, quite another.

"Guys, I've had about enough sex talk to last me a lifetime. I get it. Bear seduced you. You finally gave in. Now you're together. Simple as that. Don't need to be hearing about no hard dicks. Or naked asses. I'm good. Thanks for the visual," I groan despairingly, body shivering in disgust at the pictures floating in my brain. Icky. No more sex talk with my dad or Bear, ever again.

"See, and you wanted her to like you," Dad admonishes.

"Wha ... I ... uh ... I ... shit ... I'm sorry. I didn't mean to get carried away." Melancholy surges off Bear in strong waves.

I sit up in Dad's lap, peering over his shoulder to look at prez. He's scrubbing his beard, eyes downcast, a frown marring his features. "Hey. It's not that big of a deal. I still like you, Bear. For bein' such a badass, you sure are a softie, like Dad said."

Bear's shoulders lift and drop in a hefty shrug. "Yeah, well, it's not every day that you meet the woman who bore your grandchildren, who also happens to be the love of your life's daughter."

Yep. I think I just melted into a big puddle of pink sugary goo. He's so fucking sweet. It's no wonder Kade's his son. Not sure where Ryker came from, though. If he doesn't stop staring at me from somewhere in this dimly lit yard, my hair's liable to catch fire. At least Bear got lucky and had one decent son. Who, by my calculations, is having a damn good time getting his dick sucked. Sweet baby Jesus, who gets blowjobs out in the open like that? He's standing in front of a tree just yards away, pumping into that Janet chick's mouth. Beside that blonde is another woman on her knees, lapping at his nuts. Or, at least, I think that's what she's doing. There's not enough lighting to tell, and Janet is taking him to the root, so I can't see his length as it disappears into her throat. Either that or he's puny just like they'd joked earlier today. My guess is that's a lie. If he's anything like his brother, he's got a monster cock. Although, Janet's lips aren't about to burst at the seams. Which is a good thing. Bre—Ryker's dick ... I don't know how anyone can suck. Then again I'm sure Vanessa does a fine job. I couldn't. Some meat is just too thick to stuff into this gullet, no matter how hard I try.

Shifting me in his lap to make us more comfortable, my dad keeps me close. It may seem odd to some, considering I'm a grown woman. But once a daddy's girl, always a daddy's girl.

"Tell us more about our grandbabies," Bear requests.

And I do just that. I tell them about their favorite colors and foods. How they don't like hats, but love bandanas. That they like peanut butter sandwiches, but hate jelly. Slowly, one topic at a time, I teach them about Roxie and Scarlett, letting them get to know the two little girls who own my heart. They are my proudest accomplishment. Just as I know, I'm my father's, as evidenced by the loving gleam in his eye as he listens to me prattle on and on like a proud mama. It feels wonderful to share this with them. To reveal parts of my life that my daddy has never known, and bring Bear into the fold as their grandpa and my father's partner. I may not be over the shock of coming here and learning what I have. However, I can tell you one thing ... I wouldn't change this visit for the world. Part of me is being glued back together, bit by bit. The hole in my chest healing. Life isn't always how we want it to be, but we make do with what we've got. And I'm doing just that, right now, as I revel in the warmth spreading into my limbs, reclaiming pieces of my life that I thought were once lost.

PAST

"Oh god. Brent, that feels amazing," I groan, lost in the merriment of his thumbs massaging the arch of my foot as I soak in a lavender scented bubble bath. Yesterday, Brent brought me home this bath fizz thingy, and today, drew me a bath using it. It's flippin' divine. I wonder if he'd pick me up a few more if I asked.

Deft fingers press into the pad of my big toe, and another groan of pleasure slips free. This is too damn good. With all of the water retention I've had during my pregnancy, this is better than a hot fudge sundae on a hot summer day.

Resting my head against the back of the tub, I exhale a peaceful sigh, melting into the bliss-filled water. He spoils me so much. You'd think by now that our new relationship, honeymoon stage would be over. Doesn't that stop after a year? For us, it's going stronger than ever. Sometimes, I feel like I'm living in a dream with a perfect man, and his even perfecter body. Is that even a word? It should be. Brent's body is the epitome of perfecter.

"You're a sucker for foot massages," he teases with a smile in his voice.

"Or I'm just a sucker for yours." I blast him a sly grin, winking like a dork. In reward, he lifts my foot from the water and tenderly kisses my instep. "You're too fucking cute, babe."

A warmth skitters through me that has nothing to do with the water temperature.

Mashing my lips together, I smother my impending smile and scrub my cheeks to hide the flourishing redness. I hate that he affects me this way. That the butterflies flutter without any notice. That he can make me smile with just a single, carefree word. He's dangerous to my heart. I've known that since the moment I laid eyes on him. But I'm unable to muster enough courage to protect myself. Not when I know the reward far outweighs the possible heartache. Even if he doesn't say he loves me, I feel it in his kiss, his touch, his words. Actions speak louder than empty promises.

A whimper picks up on the baby monitor that's sitting on the vanity. "Rox must be awake." Abruptly, I sit up, grabbing the tub's edge, water sloshing up my sides. I'm ready to get out at a moment's notice if she cries.

"She'll be okay. She whimpers in her sleep all the time." Brent's calming tenor soothes my fraying nerves.

"But what if she needs me?" I pout.

"Babe," he drawls in that tone that says he thinks I'm cute for being overly paranoid. I can't help it. Being a mother has brought out a lot of things in me, this protective mama bear mentality being the most prevalent.

Brent slips a pruning hand from the water and dries it on his pant leg, darkening the denim in the process. Fishing into his front pocket, he pulls out a square, black box and rests it on the lip of the tub.

"What's that?" My sights fix on the treasure.

"It's a present for you. And I'll give it to you, only if you promise to relax and let me handle Rox if she does wake up."

Bah! I hate ultimatums. He does this almost daily. "I'll make you that tomato and mayo sandwich if you promise not to touch the dishes. I'll get to 'em later." "I've got a chocolate bar with your name on it in my glovebox if you let me take Roxie to the store with me so you can get a nap in." Sure, those sound like heavenly offers. I'd be a fool not to take them, right? Well, as easy as that sounds, a part of me loathes the idea of surrendering control. It's like this inferno burning inside me that blazes hotter when I allow someone to take care of something I feel is my duty. Mostly, it's guilt. I know this. But when I was a kid, I took care of my dad with the best of my ability, and took pride in that. So, handing over the reins is difficult, but Brent seems to know how to sway me in the right direction. It's subtle, yet effective. He's a master manipulator, and I'd be lying if I said that didn't scare me just a bit.

Sighing long and hard, I nod in acquiesce, dying to know what's hidden inside that tempting present. I love gifts. Always have. That's why Christmas is my favorite time of the year. I'm allowed to gift goodies without people looking at me funny.

The adorable smile that Brent cracks shoots straight to my heart. It's the one he reserves just for me whenever he's sublimely happy. And it makes me happy to make him happy. It works for us. We're a team. Yin and yang.

Clicking back the lid, a delicate infinity symbol rests on the soft felt attached to two thin silver strands of a necklace. It's absolutely stunning. Not too gaudy, which I don't care for. And it can be worn with everything. It's simply breathtaking. Perfect. Just for me.

Covering my mouth with dripping fingers, I "awe" behind them. "That's so pretty."

Proudly, Brent puffs his chest up. "I knew ya'd like it. Roxie helped me pick it out."

Arching a brow, I regard him like he's silly. Which he is. Roxie's a baby, barely able to crawl. "She did, did she?" I mock lightheartedly.

"She pointed, and I bought, so yeah." He snaps the box closed then sets it on the floor. "I'll put it on ya after ya get washed up."

Crooking my finger, I gesture him forward, and he complies without hesitation. Climbing onto his knees, elbows resting on the ledge of the tub, Brent leans forward and lays a sweet and savory kiss on my lips. It's soothing and makes the butterflies go berserk in my tummy as my heart strings sing a tune of love for this man. "Thank you. That was very sweet of you," I whisper against his mouth. He smiles, his steamy breath wafting intimately over my face. Goosebumps break out, shimmying down my body. I shiver, despite sitting in a hot bath.

"Anythin' you want, my little Tiger, and I'll get it for you. The infinity symbol..." Pausing, he slowly laves the seam of my lips, ripping a low, wanton moan from my soul. "...It represents how I'll always feel about you. No matter what happens. No matter what obstacles. You'll always be here." Plucking my hand from the water, he places it on his bare chest, right over his beating heart. It pounds in conviction under my palm as rivulets of water from my pruney fingers drip down his pec and onto his abs.

Hooking a damp finger under my chin, he brings my eyes up to meet his. The smoldering blue orbs glisten with emotions that I can't put my finger on. They're important. Profound. I can feel the significance pooling in my gut, even if I can't decipher what they mean. "You're always gonna be mine, Tiger. Always."

A maelstrom of unspoken words catch my tongue. Unsure of what to say, I tip my head in a single nod. "Always," I whisper, somehow sealing my fate.

PRESENT

Reseated in my camping chair, chatting with Dad, Bear, and whoever else decides to join us, I flick my wrist toward the back door. "Is there a bathroom in there that I can easily get to?"

Pushing up from the chair, Dad stands and waves me forward without saying a word, so I follow. Through the yard, people watch us until we slip into the house. Once we reach the kitchen, he stops three steps ahead of me and points to the door that dumps into the long hallway we came down earlier to eat. "At the end of the hall, there's a bathroom. It's easy to find."

I touch his arm. "You don't wanna walk me the rest of the way?"

I'm weary because Kade would have escorted me to the bathroom. Then he would have waited for me until I was done. Then again he's still tied up with that towhead for the moment. The last time I saw him, he was taking body shots from between her and one of her friends' boobs. Two other guys wearing similar leather vests had joined him. They looked like they were having way too much fun for me to intrude.

Scrubbing the back of his neck, Dad grimaces. "Uh ... I normally would, Peanut. But Scooter and Hammer are in there shootin' pool, and if I walk outta this room and they see me, they're gonna hustle me into playin'. I've been puttin' it off since last night. They're pains in the asses to deal with when they've been drinkin'. But I'll wait right here for ya to get back. Is that okay?" He looks increasingly uncomfortable asking me that. I get it. He doesn't want the headache. I wouldn't either. And I'm a big girl, anyhow. It's not like he's leaving me to fend for myself in a mysterious house.

The *clack* of pool balls drifts in from the other room. "Take that, bitch!" a man hollers.

"Fuck you, Hammer!" another replies.

Taking that as my cue, I squeeze my dad's forearm before seeing myself down the hall and through the bathroom doorway. There's a light already on. Like Kade's, it's stark white and much cleaner than I expected for this being a predominately male household. They must hire a housekeeper or something. There's no way that many men could keep this room so spotless. Surprisingly, there's not even a dribble of piss on the floor or the pungent aroma of urine. It smells like honeysuckle as I close the door and go about my business. An abundance of raucous insults funnel down the hallway, ricocheting off the walls in the half bath. I cringe at some of the less than stellar ones about being a cock sucker and lickin' somebody's mama's hairy bush. In no time, I'm washing my hands with some fancy schmancy vanilla scented soap. Yeah. Vanilla fucking soap. Talk about weird. Apparently, my preconceived biker notions are all bullshit.

Fixing flyaways with my wet fingers, I tuck a strand of hair behind my ear. I don't look half bad for having cried my eyes out less than an hour ago. Guess it's a good thing I wear waterproof mascara and eyeliner. My cheeks are rosy from the fire, which gives me a beautiful glow. If it weren't for the slight puffiness under my eyes, you wouldn't be able to tell I'd just wept. Luckily, my glasses hide most of the evidence.

Satisfied with my appearance, I yank open the bathroom door just as someone slings a racy, yo-mama joke. Head dipped, chuckling behind my hand, I walk straight into a brick wall. Or it feels that way when I bounce off, and take a stumbling step backward. A rough hand clamps around my bicep, keeping me upright, as another covers my mouth and most of my face, thanks to its size. Propelling me back into the room, he kicks the door shut with his heel, and all hell breaks loose as my fight or flight instincts kick into warp speed. Blood surging through my ears, drowning out all noise, my fingers fly of their own volition, jabbing into my assailant's throat. He coughs, almost choking, and drops his grip from my mouth to grab his neck. Powerless to stop my reflexes, my knee collides with his nuts at the same moment my fist slams into his solar plexus, spiking an inferno of pain through my fist and shoulder. Shaking my hand out, grunting through the radiant ache, my chest heaves to catch my breath. Flexing my fist, I check to make sure I didn't break any bones on the behemoth who's now incapacitated. Doubled over, collapsed onto one knee, the dumbass cups his dick and stomach while painfully dry heaving. Spittle flies from his lips with every struggled gasp.

Fuck!

I didn't ... mean to do that! Why did he have to sneak up on me, and touch me in a way that I thought he was gonna hurt me, or worse, my daughter. Son of a bitch! I ... I shouldn't have done that. And he didn't even fight back. Which is almost worse. He just let me knee him in the balls. Who allows that?

Sidestepping his crouched form in front of the door, I find space against the farthest wall that I wish I could disappear into. Which isn't far since it's so cramped, especially with him in here, sucking up all the oxygen. Sifting my hands through my hair, I tug on the blonde trusses as an avalanche of guilt consumes my brain. Shaking my head, my gut starts to churn.

No. No. No. Fuck. I may hate him, but I didn't ... I promise I didn't mean to hurt him like this.

My palm twitches, wanting to reach out and touch his shoulder, to see if there's anything I can do to make it alright. But I don't move, or say a word. I just flatten myself against the wall and suffer in silence as the guilt blasts a hole through my insides. I've never hurt anyone important before. Not that he's important. He's not. At least, not anymore. However, the boy in school who picked on me about my boobs ... he deserved the ass-whooping. My dad was so proud of me that day. And that snobby girl in high school who regularly made fun of my dad being dead.

She deserved that black eye and cooter punch. She couldn't walk straight for a week. Serves her right.

"Fuck," he finally groans, making the hairs on the back of my neck stand on end. He sounds horrible—gutted. Thank God I didn't crush his trachea. That would have been bad. Very, very bad.

Shivering as the adrenaline begins to wear off, I croak an, "I'm sorry."

Pushing himself off the floor with a grunt, Ryker slams the toilet lid closed and takes a seat on top. Resting his elbows on his knees, hunched over, hands clasped in front of him, he breathes heavily. His shoulders rise and fall with each lungful as sweat glistens on his bald head and pinched brow.

"Bre—Ryker, did you hear me? I said I was sorry." Damn it. The guilt won't stop reeling. Now my heart feels like it's shredding in my chest. To dull the pain, I rub the spot above it with my knuckle.

He expels a strained breath. "Th-there's nothing t-to apologize for." The rasp of his words are painfully hoarse. I cringe, knowing he's going to be sore for days, and it's all my fault.

"Yes, there is. I shouldn't have done that." Great. Now I'm whiny—voice ten pitches too high. I wish my hands would stop trembling.

Eyes cast on the tiled floor, Ryker shakes his head, slowly. "I deserved it." He tries to clear his throat, only it sounds like a smoker's cough. My cringe grows as I clasp my hands in front of me to stave off the shaking. It doesn't seem to work, but it's worth a try. One more second and I'm liable to reach out and touch him—to rub the sweat off his brow and pull him toward me, head resting on my belly, to comfort like old times. Sheesh, my brain sure is fucked up. My logical side knows I should feel a tiny sense of triumph for kicking his ass. While the other part of me feels irrevocably horrible. When I do something awful, I'm always trying to right my wrong. Not sure if that's a character flaw or not, but right now, it feels like one. Especially when I remind myself of all the shit he's put me through. A nut punch should be considered a walk in the park, compared to what he deserves. *Should*, being the operative word. Because I'd be lying if I said I didn't want to touch him for the sake of feeling his skin on mine, just one last time. Hate or not, there's a history there that a small sliver of me still craves. Even if I loathe that part.

"You didn't even fight back. You know how to fight. You shouldn't have let me hurt you like that." Knocking some sense into him is better than the touchy alternative. He probably won't be able to use those balls for a week. Not that I want to know if he can or not. That's just wrong.

"And what? Risk hurtin' the baby? What kinda man do you take me for?"

"The asshole variety," is on the tip of my tongue, but I suck it back for the sake of my own guilt. I don't need to feel any worse than I already do. Instead, I oust a noncommittal "huh um" sound.

Leaning back on the toilet lid, Ryker tilts his head to look at me square on. Only I refuse to garner eye contact. That's too much for me to handle with my heart racing like it is, and my gut ... well, it's not feeling so hot. Bracing his hands on his knees, he goes to stand.

"Don't move." At my command, he freezes midway. "If you wanna talk, which I'm sure ya do, then you need to stay seated." Seizing my inner boss bitch, I point a stern finger at the toilet. "You're too damn tall for me to talk to standing up. I don't want a crick in my neck. Now, please sit down."

Grumbling something profane under his breath, Ryker submits and reclaims the lid, appearing mighty pissed off. "There? Are ya happy? You never had a problem talkin' to me before. When we were—"

"We're not that way anymore," I snap. "And your height was annoying."

I'm bitter and lying through my teeth, which I hate to do. His height was one of the many things I found sexy about him. Presently, it just gives me another reason to hate him for being so damned attractive. It's quite disturbing how the one person in the world you're most attracted to physically, you can't stand emotionally. I shift from one foot to the other as the truth agitates my stomach, and the shaking finally wears off.

Elbows re-perched on his knees, fingers tightly clasped together in obvious frustration, Ryker's narrowed eyes focus in my direction. I hate to admit it, but that searing heat they exude is causing my skin to prickle. I can't explain how it works. Perhaps it's some psychological problem I've got. Though I swear they're like a laser beam. I can physically feel them roam, land, and roam some more, never leaving my body as they scorch a trail of heat in their wake. It's eerie.

"You don't have to be a bitch to get your point across, Tiger," he grumbles.

My hands occupy themselves by rubbing my belly in circles. It's the perfect distraction. "If you want me to be nice, then I suggest you stop using that nickname."

"You already knocked my fucking nuts into my stomach. What else do ya want? I'm not gonna stop using a nickname I gave you. So you're just gonna have to deal with that shit."

Great. Now I've got a fiery ex to handle. I liked him better when he was incapacitated. At least then he couldn't talk, and those gorgeous eyes weren't looking at me in ways that I can't make out, and don't care to try and decipher.

Harrumphing, I glare at his chin. It's a nice chin with a thick goatee and ruggedly sharp angle. One that I used to bite during sex. Oh, fucking, jeez. Why am I thinking about that? Shit ... okay ... I sweep my glare to his shoulder ... the perfect place to dig my nails into when he was screwing me hard. Oh ... My ... God... This is so wrong. Why am I thinking about sex? *Uh!* Blinking rapidly, I banish the lewd thoughts from my brain and stare at the wall above his head. If I look at him, I'm going to pay too much attention to that stupidly sexy body and those tattoos he never had before we met. And trust me, there's plenty of them that my dirty little mind would like to explore with my tongue. If I didn't hate him, that is.

"Listen, babe, you shouldn't be here. I dunno why Pops was stupid enough to allow it. But this ain't right. You need to leave, and soon. "

Hell no! My arms fold right across my chest, tucking in annoyance. "You don't have any say in what I do or don't do anymore. So I suggest you try a different tactic. Like, stop ordering me around. I'm not the same woman you were with a million years ago. I've got a backbone. And I sure as fuck ain't gonna let some deadbeat ex of mine tell me what to do. You've got ten seconds to explain what the hell you want, or I'm out." There. That should work. He better listen.

Sighing, he then garbles something unintelligible. Yep, he's irritated, just as much as I am. Good. "I'm not yankin' your chain, Kat. Pops bringin' ya here is gonna put heat on the club if anyone finds out. Ghost is supposed to be dead. And the people after him won't like it if they find out otherwise. He can't travel outside of town for his and the club's safety. Bringin' ya here is puttin' all my girls in danger."

"Well, I'm sorry that I'm causin' problems for your precious Vanessa. Roxie and Scarlett are none of your damn business," I snip.

"Woman!" Ryker shoots off the lid so fast he's a blur. A heartbeat later and his hot, rock-hard body is pressed against mine, breathing labored, eyes wild as they peer down at me from his intimidating height. His lip curls in aggression as I freeze, shocked to my core that he's so close that I can smell him. T-to-touch him. Oh shit.

"I am not talkin' about Vanessa. I'm talkin' about you and my daughters." His colossal hand splays itself on the wall beside my head, caging me in. The other drops on top of my belly. Eyes flying wide, my heart rockets into my throat. What the hell is going on? A flutter emerges that I once thought was dead. Oh ... no ... this is not acceptable.

Regathering my wits, I shove his hand off my baby bump, and he lets it fall to the wayside. "You don't get to touch my daughter," I hiss, placing my palms on his wide shoulders. The leather of his vest is surprisingly soft. "Get away from me." I shove with all my might, and it does nothing. Not a flinch or sway. I hate that he's so huge. *Gah!*

Ryker snorts. "I like you right where I've got ya. So I'm not fuckin' movin', my little Tiger."

Fan-fucking-tastic. Now the jerkoff is amused. Not what I was going for.

Scowling, brows pinched to the point I might get a headache, I slap his unforgiving chest, ignoring the sting that claims my palm. "You don't get to call me your anything, motherfucker."

"Sure I do. You're not gonna try to kick my ass again, 'cause you'll feel too guilty, and I like bein' this close to you."

Stupid, smug, son of a bitch!

"You're not God's gift to women, Brent! Ryker! Uh! Whatever the hell your name is."

He leans in and audibly sniffs my hair.

Oh no, he didn't!

He doesn't get to smell me! He doesn't get anything from me! Putting my back into it, I strain to push him away again. It's hopeless. Nada.

Grinding my teeth, I seethe, "Stop sniffing my fucking hair."

"I missed the way you smell," he whispers, hot breath fanning over my scalp.

Does he not understand I'm angry as hell? Can't he feel the rage boiling inside of me as I begin to vibrate? If he's not careful, I'm gonna unleash on him again, and this time, I won't stop. Damn it. Why does he do this to me? Does he like pushing my buttons? I can usually keep my cool. Right now, it's impossible. He brings out the worst in me.

"I didn't miss a damn thing about your ugly ass," I lie.

"Don't be so hateful, babe. My ass ain't ugly." Always with the jokes. Well, this isn't funny. I'm not laughing. 'The Hulk' is about to burst out of my chest any second and smash him into the ground.

"Ha, ha," I deadpan, curling my hands into fists atop his pecs, on the verge of socking him in that perfect jaw.

"Come on. Let it all out," he urges.

What the hell is he talking about?

"What?" I clip.

"Let it out. Say what you wanna say. Tell me how much of a piece of shit I am. How I was a dick for leaving you. How I'm the worst father in the world. That I don't deserve to breathe in the same room as you. Say it. I know you're thinkin' it. Everybody is. Come on. What are ya waitin' for?"

Is he serious? Sure, that's what I want to say, but he just took all the fun out of it. And his self-deprecating tone is almost painful to listen to. Especially with the raspy edge that's only there because I jabbed him in the neck. Talk about making me feel like a complete jerk and zapping my rage from a million miles an hour to zero in a matter of seconds. What a buzz kill.

"Whatever." Dropping my hands to my sides, stiff as a board, I bite my inner cheek.

Giving me a smidge of my bubble back, Ryker stops sniffing my hair yet doesn't move away. "What? You don't wanna cuss me out? Tell me I'm the biggest piece of shit you've ever known? I know ya do, babe. I've already been ripped a new asshole from Ghost. The man can't even talk to me without losin' his shit. The worst part is: I don't blame him. I'd feel the same way if it was my daughter some prick had fucked over." He pauses like he's waiting for me to say something. Only, I've got nothing to say. I'm not sure if he wants my sympathy, or truly expects me to lay into him. He's an infuriating conundrum. I'll give him that.

A dense silence stretches between us, making me all too aware of our closeness, and the spicy scent of his skin. The way his chest rises and falls as he respires too deeply is distracting enough that I can nearly overlook the monster sized erection that's pressing into my belly, branding its memory there. I can't believe he could be hard at a time like this. Not with me, his ex. And certainly not after I pummeled his nuts minutes ago.

Fidgeting, I struggle to keep my emotions in check. Inhaling and exhaling controlled breaths, I stay calm, refusing to let him get to me. I'm better than that.

His other hand settles on the wall next to my shoulder as I continue to stare at the center of his chest. "When are you due?"

"That's none of your business."

I will not overreact. I will not tell him the truth. I will successfully lie until the guilt truly eats a hole through my soul and I drop dead. My lapse in judgment months ago was not my finest moment. It was an awful man who exploited my weakness and used it to his advantage. He offered me everything, only to rip it away after a tiny taste. Then, one morning weeks later, I woke up puking my guts out. That was when I knew my lapse in judgment was gonna cost me dearly. Not only emotionally, but financially, as I became a mother for the third time.

"When is Vanessa due?" I counter, keeping my tone light—unaffected.

"February sometime."

Oddly enough, he doesn't sound too thrilled about that. Maybe it's because he's still sporting wood for some ungodly reason, or talking to me about it. It has to be awkward speaking to the mother of your children about your wife having a baby. I know it's not the easiest thing for me to hear, but at least this child will have a mom and a dad to care for him or her. As bitter as I am about Ryker being a deadbeat dad, I don't wish a fatherless childhood on any kid. Even his unborn baby. On that same token, I'm not gonna lie and say it doesn't hurt some. 'Cause it does. It brings up a whole shit ton of insecurities that I refuse to dwell on any longer. I've spent far too many years absorbed in those darker feelings, and thought I'd gotten over them ... until recently.

"That's nice," I reply, keeping my optimistic mask in place.

"I'm not here to talk about her," Ryker grumbles. "I wanna know when you're due."

His hips swivel, rubbing his erection along my belly like he can't help himself. It shouldn't feel as nice as it does, and my clit shouldn't be reacting like it is. I can't help it when I'm forced to bite back a groan. For years, I prayed that his cock would catch some incurable STD, turn green, and fall off. Apparently, my wishes didn't come true. Half of me is sad about that, while the naughtier half is reveling in the feel of it. *Stupid, traitorous body.*

It's time to call a spade a spade so he'll stop focusing on my daughter, and with any luck, give me a moment's reprieve. "Why are you hard, Ryker? You're married. You shouldn't be rubbing your dick on your ex. That's pretty disrespectful."

"You're pregnant," he states as if that explains it all. It doesn't.

Tipping my head way back, I officially meet his gaze. Staring at his chest did nothing to help my libido. Not that his striking eyes are much better. "Yeah. So?" I remark, full of sass.

"You know what you bein' pregnant does to me. Hell. What *you* do to me. You're too fuckin' beautiful for your own damn good." There's so much honesty in his face it's impossible to ignore.

"You need to stop talking right now, and take a step back. You've lost your mind." I muster the best glower I'm able, even though it's pointless. My words won't penetrate his thick skull. And I'd be lying if I said there weren't butterflies in my stomach doing the goddamn polka. Compliments from him shouldn't feel as good as they do. I hate this bastard! This isn't fair. Why hasn't my body gotten the memo that we don't like him? My mind comprehends that. My body ... it's ... fuck ... he's already making me wet. And those tender blue eyes are drawing me like a moth to a flame. Just like they used to all those years ago. I squeeze them shut to break the connection, but it's too late, my heart is already in it. My nipples grow hard as a shiver passes through me that has nothing to do with being cold. A boulder of shame settles in my soul for getting excited. I'm going to go to hell for this I just know it. He's going to ruin me more than he already has.

"That was lost the day I left you, and I haven't gotten it back since," he replies.

"You're bein' stupid." Eye's closed, I push his shoulders. It's weak at best. "Now back away, before..."

"Before what?" Ryker's massive frame leans firmly against mine, his heavy breath washing over my face. Wanton heat blooms in my gut as my panties soak through. What's wrong with me?

My hands that haven't left his shoulders begin to tremble, even as I try to stop them.

"Before I—"

Lips brutally crashing down on mine rob me of speech. Everything in my world short circuits as Ryker breaches my mouth with his hungry tongue. A growl rattles in his chest, and he grabs my ass, drawing my hips to him as he thrusts his hardened cock against my belly. My fingers slip into his vest, and I dig my nails into his meaty pecs over his shirt, loving the grunt he expels.

Impatiently, his tongue coaxes mine, tempting me to kiss back. I remain still, allowing him to plunder wet and greedily without joining along. It's tough, but I'm trying to be strong, even if I have to throttle a needy whimper when he extracts his tongue to taste the seam of my lips—knowing just what I like.

"Kiss me back, babe. I can feel ya shaking. I know you need this as much as I do."

Hooking my leg over his hip, he affectionately nudges my nose with his before peppering kisses across my cheeks, along my jaw, and back to my mouth where he tastes my lips with the sweep of his tongue—enticing me to break, to fall victim to his delicious charms. And, fuck it all, I want to so badly. Just one last time. Consequences be damned.

Exhaling unsteadily, I shake my head. "I ... I can't."

Not taking no for an answer, the stubborn brute seizes my other leg, forcing me to wrap myself around his hips, ankles locking above his ass. Clasping my hands behind his neck for support, my pussy settles over his thickness, and he thrusts, hitting my clit on the first try. A spark of ecstasy sizzles in my blood as I toss my head back, hitting the wall, groaning in my throat as he does it again and again, relentlessly shocking my system.

Nails piercing the nape of his neck, I cry out. "You should stop."

"No. I wanna make you come," Ryker growls, painfully gripping my cheeks and rocking his pelvis in slow, steady strokes, knowing damn well what's going to make me burst. My skin feels too tight. My body a liquid firestorm as he brings me closer and closer to the brink of no return. Whimpers of madness fall from my lips. Eyes roll into the back of my head as the blinding pleasure increases, driving me insane.

"Oh god," I moan, rolling my own hips to gain better purchase.

I'm almost there.

"That's it," he rasps. "Take what you need."

"I fucking hate you." And I do. I can't believe he's doing this to me. Turning me inside out. Feeding this insatiable hunger that I've only ever felt for him, regardless of my intense hatred.

"I know ya do. Now it's time to come."

Knowing how to pluck my body like a guitar string, Ryker moves my hips up and down his length, faster and faster until my clit screams for mercy. Giving none, he slams my back against the wall, careful of my belly, and everything in my world detonates. Screaming through the torrent of raw pleasure tearing me limb from limb, my body quakes, losing itself to his onslaught. Lips crash down on mine, swallowing my cries, and I kiss back.

Ravenously, our tongues collide, fighting for supremacy as I ride the aftermath of bliss through its crests and fizzles.

Not finished, Ryker continues to fuck my little button until I can't take it anymore. Ripping my lips from his with a gasp, he immediately dives in for more. "Stop, you asshole."

Panting, he pecks the corner of my mouth. "Give me your lips, my little Tiger."

I turn my head away, and his lips brush my cheek in the most delicious of ways.

Oh God. What have I done?!

A tsunami of guilt floods in.

"No. We shouldn't have done that." I try to wiggle out of his arms, and unhook my ankles to get down, but he doesn't let me go. I slap his chest in frustration. "Put me down, Ryker. We shouldn't do this. You're married, and the biggest fucking asshole on the planet!"

Bracketing me with one arm to keep me from falling, he slips his other hand between our bodies, into the top of my leggings and panties, where he glides two fingers inside my pussy. It happens so fast that I jolt in his arms as my eyes blow wide. Goosebumps flare over every square inch of my body.

I ... I can't believe...

Oh yes...

Stilling, he presses a gentle kiss to my lips, and it takes everything within me not to kiss him back. Seriously, what the fuck is wrong with me?!

I bite his bottom lip instead. It's not meant for foreplay. It's in warning. "Take your fingers out of my pussy!" I roar.

"Why?" He toys with my g-spot, and it takes every ounce of energy not to moan. *Cocky fucking dickhead!*

"Because I hate you! You lied to me repeatedly, and I don't want you touching me!"

"You're wet for me, baby. I know you might hate me, but your body doesn't." He's not funny. He's serious. The gleam in his eye tells me he hates how I feel about him, but that he relishes in the fact that my body is a slave to his. I hate that about myself. It makes me feel like a cheap whore.

Powerless to stop, I slap him clear across the face. It's cruel as it echoes in the small room, and dispels a fraction of my self-loathing. Why do I always let him in? Why do I like it when he touches me? I ... god ... I hate it. All of it. I shouldn't want him like I do. I shouldn't be thinking about how his dick would feel ten times better in place of his fingers. I shouldn't be getting wetter at the prospect. This is so disgusting. I'm sick and depraved. I need help.

"Hit me again," he urges, and I glare, lips pursed.

"What the hell? Why would you want me to slap you again?"

"Because it'll make you feel better." He's as calm as can be aside from his labored breathing, which I'm sure has nothing to do with anger and everything to do with how hard his dick is. Dipping his head, he offers his bottom lip to me. "Bite me. Take out your anger. Make me pay for what I did to you. Use me. I

145

don't fucking care, my little Tiger. Just make yourself feel better." Sincerity steeps his words and obliterates every ounce of my restraint.

One second, I'm seething, and the next, I'm biting his lip and sucking it into my mouth as he groans his approval. Carefully setting me on my feet, he pulls away just long enough to tear my leggings and panties down my legs in one fell swoop. I don't know what possess me, but I hold onto his shoulders and step out of them without hesitation. As reward, he presses a chaste kiss to my lips, then lays down on the tiled floor, knees bent. Unzipping his pants, he extracts the most beautiful monster cock from its denim prison. Springing into the air, a dribble of pre-cum rolls down his bulbous cockhead, onto his shaft.

Fisting the base of his manhood, Ryker waves me forward. "Ride me." He smears the clear liquid into his skin using his thumb.

Back against the wall, trembling with a surplus of pent-up emotions, I frantically shake my head. There's no way I'm fucking him. Kissing is one thing. But screwing is what got me into this mess in the first place. Bending down, I go to grab my clothes to put them back on, but Ryker is faster. He seizes my hips and drags me to him like I'm weightless. Forcing me to straddle him, he positions himself at my entrance and thrusts upward to breach my core before I can scramble away. *Holy fuck!* Tossing my head toward the sky, I moan at the fullness. I can't help it. I don't want to like it, but I do. I love it so damn much.

His cockhead resting just inside my pussy, I shove the flaps of his vest apart and shuck his t-shirt up his rippled abs to expose his pecs. Without a second thought, I sink my long nails into the meat, and he moans so loudly that I almost come on the spot. Eyes rolling back into his skull, chest driving upward toward my fingers like he wants me to hurt him more, he digs his own digits into my curvy hips, but not too hard that I'll bruise.

"More," he chokes, swollen lips parted, gasping.

"You want me to hurt you?" I rake my nails down his chest, loving the red streamers they leave in their wake.

"I want you to make me pay. I deserve it." Holding my hips, he glides me back down his shaft to the hilt. It aches from being stuffed so fully, but it doesn't take long for me to adjust.

Slowly, I trace a nail around his pierced nipples. They were never that way when we were together. It's sexy. The silver barbells are a stark contrast against his tan skin, and make my mouth water, eager to suck. Biting my bottom lip, I flick the barbell with my nail, and he shudders, ousting a groan. I do it again for good measure and his hips lurch. This could be fun—torturing him because of all the shit he's done to me. To show him who's in charge. To make him weep with the need to come. The prospect is rather enticing.

Reaching behind me, I cup his balls in my palm. He sucks a pained breath. "These are gonna be sore for a few days," I remark, squeezing and rolling them just slightly to make his eyes bulge and thighs quake.

"They already fuckin' hurt," he grouses.

"And why is that?"

147

"'Cause I couldn't leave you alone like I was supposed to." Ryker's hands securing my waist begin to tremble, and his abs contract, tightening the stupidly gorgeous ridges, all eight of them. A mistiness glazes across his heavy-lidded eyes.

Swiveling my hips, I bask in the feel of him hitting deep. "And why couldn't you do that? Huh? You had no problem abandoning your daughters..." *And me.*

"'Cause you fuckin' own me."

Anger spikes in my heart at his barefaced lie. I don't own anything of his. If I did, he wouldn't have done all that he has. Slashing my nails across his abs in retribution, I lift myself off his cock, only to slam back down again. We both cry out, so I fuck him harder, riding his dick, impaling myself on the only cock I've ever had. Fingers embedding in his chest, I take what I want, rejoicing in the power and delicious satisfaction. Each stroke bottoms out, cracking the foundation of my pain as my clit rubs against the dusting of coarse hair above his manhood.

Lost to sensation, I let everything go. Moans and groans of unadulterated ecstasy pour from my lips as I pleasure myself using him like he used me. Just like he deserves. "I fucking hate you so much," I cry out as he thrusts upward at the same moment I drive down, meeting in a beautifully raw connection that delivers a shot of bliss straight into my g-spot, nearly sending me over.

Damn!

Ryker knives up and maneuvers my legs so they curl around his waist, and we're flush together, my belly molded against his, our lips a hairsbreadth apart. He pushes my hair over my shoulder, opening my neck up for him to feast on, and so he does. Licking and sucking there, he rocks our pelvises together, driving me mad.

"Why did you ... have to break my... Oh ... God..." He nibbles beneath my ear, and I dig my heels into his bare ass. Just a little more. I just need a little bit more...

"You're close. I can feel it," he growls.

Clenching my walls around him, I rasp a shaky, "Y-yes."

Ryker slides his cock out of my pussy, only to fuck me harder on the down stroke. "Take what you want, beautiful. Take it. Make yourself come," he demands. "Fuckin' take it. Come all over my dick."

Coiling tighter and tighter, I quickly stave off my orgasm, not wanting to give it to him yet. "No," I bark, slamming our bodies as one. The sloppy sounds of our coupling mixed with the scent of sex makes me groan. Stuffing my face into the crook of his neck, I bite him there, sinking my teeth in hard enough to leave a mark.

Mmmm ... his skin tastes good. Just like I remember.

"Fuck, Kat. That's it. You're gonna make me lose it."

Oh hell no. He does not get to come. Not before I finish the second time. Leaning back just enough, I wrap my fingers around his throat and squeeze at the same moment I bury his cock to the hilt and still, refusing to let him spill into me just yet. Not that I should let him come at all. He's not worthy of that. Not anymore.

A satisfied rumble vibrates in his chest as if he's totally okay with me refusing him. Perhaps he's just as fucked in the head as I am.

Lifting my mouth to his, fingers still on his throat, I tease his parted lips with the wet tip of my tongue. "You're not coming. This isn't about you. You're the asshole who left your kids and me. You chose your club over us. You don't get to come. You don't get a fuckin' thing from me, you asshole."

"I am an asshole. Your asshole." His voice is gravelly, strained. It only makes me hotter, wanting to do nastier, naughtier things to him. Things we used to do when we first met. But that can't happen.

"You're not mine. Not anymore." It hurts to admit that aloud. I've never said it before. Not to anyone. Tears well in my eyes, but I refuse to let them run over. So I briefly close them instead to wash away the melancholy before it consumes me. Then release his throat.

Kissing my top lip, Ryker then pushes his hands between our bodies and pulls a gold band off his left ring finger. I'd never noticed it there before, but it makes sense that he'd wear one since he's married. See, I'm such a homewrecker. Why am I doing this?

Spreading his fingers, he motions his chin toward them. "Look at my ring finger."

I do, and what I see has my heart leaping into my throat as I gasp a noiseless breath. *My initials.* Ryker has my initials on the inside of his ring finger. He tilts his hand so I can see the other side, and there, inked into his flesh, is my birthdate.

I open my mouth to ask him why would he do such a thing, but he beats me to it. "Six months after I left, I was going insane and at everybody's throats, fighting with Ghost every damn day. I started hittin' the bottle hard to dull the pain. Then one day, Pops told me he was takin' me to get my first tattoo. Said it was better therapy than drinkin' myself to death. That's when I got these." He wiggles his ring finger.

Uh ... Wow ... Just ... Wow...

"That was your first tattoo?" I ask in awe.

"Yeah; it was. But my artist touches it up for me every year so it doesn't fade."

That's oddly sweet, kind of romantic, and also a bit painful. He didn't care to do that when we were together, yet it was important afterward. He doesn't make any damn sense. Who does that?

"And what does Vanessa think about that?" I'd be pissed if my husband had another woman's initials and birthday under our wedding band.

Ryker shrugs one shoulder as if he doesn't give a crap. "I dunno. Never asked." Tossing his ring on the floor, it *clinks* then *tinkles* as it slides to a stop. Curling his fingers under the hem of my shirt, he drags it over my belly and sets his big mitt on top of the bump. The urge to shove it away is great, but I let it go for now. "So, when's my daughter due?" he tests, raising a serious brow, his still-hard cock flexing in my pussy.

"W-what?" I stammer, then clear my throat, forcing my expression to remain neutral.

151

Tenderly caressing my stretch mark littered belly, he absentmindedly traces hearts and other designs across the ruined skin as he stares at my face. "You heard me. When is my daughter due?"

"I don't know what you're talking about," I lie, knowing exactly what he's talking about, but not wishing to discuss it.

"Come on, Kat. Don't play me for some fool. You gotta be due in March. I already know how far along you are."

"How do you know that?" I croak.

"Because I know a lot more about you than ya think."

Huffing, I narrow my eyes at him so he knows I'm not playing. "What is that supposed to mean?"

"That means, the night I showed up to your house at two in the morning, and we had sex on your back patio, I know I knocked you up." He's way too composed to be having this conversation. How could he possibly know that? He couldn't. I didn't mean to let my guard slip. I swear. I didn't mean for that encounter to happen.

Sleeping peacefully next to Derek, my boyfriend of almost five months, I'd gotten up to use the restroom and grab a bite of chocolate from the kitchen. There was a knock at the door that startled me from my late night snacking. I can't help it. It's always been one of my secret addictions. Chocolate at four in the morning is pretty normal for me. When I'd heard the shallow raps, I peered through the peephole, and my heart literally sputtered to a stop. With an unsteady hand, I'd cracked the door open to see what in the hell Brent was doing at my house looking haggard. He appeared like he hadn't slept in weeks, and his gaunt, overgrown face was sharper than I remembered, even if he'd bulked up everywhere else. Shoulders filling out his t-shirt to max capacity gave me the perfect outline of his pecs under the glow of the moonlight. He was a sight to behold. One that tipped my world upside down in a matter of seconds.

To keep from going into too much detail, let's just say Brent decided to play games with not only my head but my heart that night. He'd begged me to come outside. Told me he was sorry for everything. That he'd made a mistake, and was moving back to make things right again. He'd even gotten teary eyed. I fell for it like a damned fool and went to comfort him, telling him that we'd figure something out. I was trying to be the bigger person and not let my shattered past cloud my judgment. I'd come a long way over the years, and slowly began to accept the loss. But that night, he'd torn everything asunder. My emotions were jumping like a pogo stick all over the place. My body was unstable, shifting from goosebumps to trembling and sometimes a mix of the two. I was half-awake and an utter mess. However, regardless of my inner turmoil, I'd still sought to make everything better for him. To whisper sweet nothings in his ear like years hadn't passed, and we were back to the time when we were happy together. One thing had led to another, and he'd kissed me. It tasted of desperation, and I tried to say no, but the words died a thousand deaths on my lips. I couldn't seem to tear myself away no matter how hard I tried.

Everything operated on autopilot, including my hopeful heart.

Succumbing to the heat of the moment, we'd made love on the patio table in my backyard. And when I say made love, that's what it felt like. It was gentle and deliberate. He drew out all of my orgasms, one right after the other. Every part of me melted into a puddle of relief and happiness being in his arms again. He'd even came twice, filling me to the brim. When it was all said and done, he'd promise to contact me once the girls had woken up so we could attempt to repair what he'd broken. And like the stupid, optimistic woman I am, I believed him. Even my gut believed him without signaling a single twinge of warning.

Not caring one iota that I would have to break Derek's heart in the morning, I'd fallen asleep on the couch with the biggest smile on my face and Brent's cum deep inside me, right where I felt it belonged. Little did I know that my happiness would be short-lived. One day turned into two and then three, and I soon realized that I'd been duped, played for a fool. The scars that had long healed splintered, leaving them just as raw as the day he left. I cried for a week and didn't tell a soul about what had happened. A few weeks later, when the nausea started, I knew his super sperm had spun its magic once more.

My daughters and mother have repeatedly asked who the father is. However, I've been too much of chicken to admit my shortcomings. Especially since Roxie and Scarlett don't deserve to be hurt by the news that their father dropped by one mysterious evening and now their mother is pregnant. As far as they know, it was a guy I dated, even if I've never slept with a single one of them—it never felt right. I mean ... what was I supposed to say? What would you do? Would you have told them all the truth? It's not like I enjoy lying. But if it saves my girls from heartache, I've got to try and protect them, right?

Resting my palms on his relaxed shoulders, I focus on what I want to know. Screw his questions. "Did you know I was pregnant before I got here?"

"Yes." It's monotone.

Of course, he did. With the volume of deceitful things he's done, this shouldn't surprise me.

"Did you think she was yours?"

Looking away, he says nothing. Though his guilt-stricken features are confession enough.

Gripping his chin, I turn his eyes back to mine and hold him there. "What else do you know that you're not tellin' me?"

"Nothing," he mumbles, lying all over again and pissing me off.

Arg! I'm sick and freaking tired of being someone's plaything. Hell, he probably had every intention of breaking in here to sleep with me. And being the gullible, dumbass that I am, I believed him when he proffered his body as a whipping post to ease my hatred. And what did I do? I didn't walk out, or slap him, or beat his ass some more, despite my guilt. No; I allowed him to manipulate me. And I'm too damn stupid to see that I'm just another pawn in his sick and twisted games. What an idiot I've been. Falling for it, and allowing his cock inside of me where it's always felt at home. Even if that in itself is the biggest boldfaced lie of them all. Home. Sheesh, what a joke. He's a player to rival them all. He doesn't care about me. If he did, he wouldn't have done the shit he's done over and over and over again. Will I ever learn? I sure as hell hope so.

Ousting a frustrated huff, I unhook my legs from around his waist, plant my bare feet on the cold tile floor and try to stand, using his shoulders as leverage. Only, I barely budge an inch, if that, when those bulging arms of his lock around my middle as his half-hard member slips from my pussy.

"Please don't leave," he half begs, sounding unexpectedly sincere.

An infuriated grumble rolls up my throat, and I slap his shoulders, blasting two more shots of pain up my arms. "Are you fucking kidding me?" I snip.

"You're angry with me again? I thought we were over that. Why are you mad now?"

"Because I was stupid enough to sleep with you against my better judgment. You mess with my head, and you know it. Now you lie to me again. Are you ever going to stop playin' with me? I'm not just some notch in your belt. I'm a human being."

Ryker snorts a humorless laugh, arms still locked around me. "*I* mess with your head? That's rich. Really fuckin' rich, Kat. 'Cause you've been fuckin' with my head since the moment I laid eyes on you."

"Liar!" Wiggling in his embrace, losing my shit, I try to get away. It's futile. It always is. *Gah!*

"I'm not a liar. I'm being honest with you!"

"No. You're not. You won't tell me how you know things. Or what you know. Then you expect me to just spill my guts to you. I'm not doing that again, Bre—Ryker. Not after all this shit I've been through."

"If I tell you, Kat, You'll never wanna speak to me again."

"I've barely spoken to you in years, anyhow! So why do you care?"

"Because, I never stopped caring about you!" Great. Now we're officially screaming in each other's face.

"Gee. That's wonderful. Great. Fantastico. You still care. Well, let me clue you in on a little something, you big over-muscly-boy." I jab my finger into his unforgiving chest, trying not to snap a bone. "You can care about someone all you fucking please. But actions always speak louder than words. And since your actions suck some major donkey nuts, I could give two rats' asses if you cared or not."

"I know you're pregnant with my child because I had someone talk to Derek," he blurts, and everything inside of me coalesces into an atomic bomb to rival all others. Exploding, it sends me into a frenzy.

"You did what?!" I shriek, banging on his chest with my fists like a gorilla. It's not hard enough to hurt him, but loud enough that the resounding thuds sound like someone's being killed in here as I curse him up one side and down the other, spewing the F-word like a trucker.

Take that, you shithead. The side of my fist collides with his collar bone. Then another and another land haphazardly any place I can connect.

Patiently, Ryker sits motionless and lets me run out of steam.

Exhausted, heaving for oxygen, my arms burning from exertion, sweat streaming down my cheeks and clinging to the edges of my hair, I lazily deliver my last punch. It's pathetic and aches something fierce. "F-fuck you, you stupidly good-looking asshole," I wheeze, slumping against his chest, cheek resting over his sturdy heart. Curling his protective arms around my back, palms resting just above my butt, he holds me close, kissing the top of my damp head.

"I-I don't like you," I utter.

Slipping a hand up my back, combing his fingers through my long trusses, Ryker gives me a moment, or ten, to recover. "We've got surveillance cameras on your house twenty-four-seven to make sure you're safe, Kat. I installed them the week I left. Which is what I'd been sent there to do in the first place, after doin' a little recon. That's the truth..."

Sighing long and hard, he pauses a beat, then continues on as I sit here in stunned silence, my arms tucked in front of me, enjoying the warmth of his gentle embrace. "Ghost watches the videos, and the junk tapes get erased. I steal them sometimes to watch. And I have a guy on the inside named Bulk. He's a club brother. We go way back. He and his old lady just moved a few towns over from you. His woman, Jezebel, has been tapin' all the girls' dance recitals for me since she put their daughter in the class, too. And before that, a chick named Candy Cane was doin' it. I've been keepin' tabs for years. Right along with your dad. I'm not lyin' to you on purpose, babe. I just didn't want you to know..."

Holy ... Wow...

I don't know that to say. This is some CIA crazy mafia shit.

"Every boyfriend you've had, I'd send a local brother there to scope out. If I thought he was a douche, I made sure we'd send 'em packin'. If he was alright, I'd let it ride a few months to see how shit played out. Didn't like ya with other men. Pissed me the fuck off. But I also didn't want you alone, and heartbroken, either..."

"So there ya have it... you wanted to know the truth. I never stopped carin', my little Tiger. And 'cause I was afraid of the shit parade that might rain down on you if I stayed, I left. It's not 'cause I didn't fuckin' wanna be there. *Jesus.* I've wanted to be there, wakin' up next to you, for the rest of my goddamn life. But the same reason you shouldn't be here is the same reason I bailed. Not 'cause of the club. But my connections to the club. My pops has been prez for as long as I can remember. People know him, and bein' his son, they know me, too. In our circles, I can't fly under the radar out in the open, exposed like that. And neither can Ghost. That's why we live in BF-fuckin'-E, and we're smart about it. Gotta be. The guys who your dad fucked over are still around. They already got beef with our club. We're rivals. All it takes is one misstep, and we're goin' to war. And I didn't want you gettin' pulled into that life. Didn't want that for my girls either. If they caught wind of me bein' Bear's son, and datin' Mike Remington's daughter, they could start askin' questions. Stirrin' shit up. Turnin' over rocks to see what they can find. Then you and our girls would be caught in the crossfire. Dragged into a mess you didn't create and shouldn't be punished for. I'm sorry, but I couldn't live with that."

Snuggling my nose into his warmth, I inhale his distinct, manly scent. A blooming heat soothes the depths of my soul from the comfort of his smell more than it ever has before. Perhaps that's because we're finally laying all the cards on the table. He's being honest, and I'm drained from pounding all my pent up animosity into his pecs. I hate that my emotions are all over the place. I'd blame it on pregnancy hormones, but I can't be sure that's where they're coming from.

"Can I ask you some questions?" I whisper.

"You can ask me whatever you want to, babe. I'll tell ya whatever I can, within reason." His tone is feather soft—loving. The growing warmth expands into my limbs, all the way down to my toes. Wanting to be closer to him as I wrap my brain around his confessions, I slip my hand up his shirt and lay my palm flat on his abs. Gasping a sharp breath, they flex under my attention, hot and damp to the touch.

"Am I really in danger bein' here?"

"I'm not sure. But Pops shoulda thought about that before he let you come. He's not a reckless man. So I'm gonna say he took precautions before givin' ya the go ahead. We haven't talked about it since you got here. I've been too busy fightin' with Ghost and Vanessa to get a chance to have a sit down with him. If he didn't, we're gonna have problems. I don't think he would've put all of us at risk if he wasn't certain he had all possible threats on lockdown."

This is like a mob movie come to life. Except it's a motorcycle club. I'm living in a total Twilight Zone here. I mean, I'm a librarian with two daughters. Not some hardass biker chick. Not that I'm weak, I'm not. But this is far beyond my area of expertise. Sure, I've read fictional books about this lifestyle. Tille Cole has a whole series built around some badass biker club that has it out for a religious cult. The main character Styx has been one of my all-time book boyfriends for a while. What can I say? He's dreamy. And now, here I am, seated in my half-naked ex's lap, who's covered in tattoos, and talking about a life I've only read about. It's surreal as hell. As if finding out my dad was alive wasn't shocking enough, now I've got this whole new layer I've got to grasp. And let's be honest, shall we, I'm not sure how I'm supposed to understand it. Do you?

"O-kay," I drawl. "So you've been fighting with Vanessa?" I change the subject away from the club stuff because I don't feel like dwelling on the potential danger any more than I have to. Because what can I do to change it anyhow? Nothing. It'll just get me worked up, and I've already burnt the wick at both ends. I'm downright exhausted.

"I don't want—" There's a double bang at the door, disrupting Ryker's words.

"Your time is up, brother," Kade says.

What's going on here? I thought Kade was on my side, not Ryker's. Something smells awfully fishy.

"We're almost done," Ryker replies. "Just give us a few more minutes."

"I've already run interference with Ghost and Pops twice. They're gonna start gettin' antsy, and Vanessa just drove up. So if you wanna keep a lid on your little bathroom tango, I suggest you get dressed and get the fuck outta here before shit really hits the fan."

"Fuck," Ryker hisses, then hooks his finger under my chin, bringing my head up. He presses a sweet and supple kiss to my lips, lingering it there for a moment. "I'm sorry, beautiful, but we gotta jet. If you want me to finish ya, I can real quick." His nose nuzzles the corner of mine.

I sigh, saddened by the sudden burst of our Ryker-Katrina bubble.

"I know. It sucks. I wanted to talk to ya some more, and do other things," he whispers.

"This doesn't change anything between us."

My heart cracks down the center as I speak those gut wrenching words. I have to let him go for the second time. Part of me knows it's the right thing. Though deep down, I'm clinging to what once was. I wish I wasn't so blinded by past love. Love that's dust in the wind by now. We have different lives. But after our talk, I feel a little better about parting ways. At least I know what we had was real. That he does care for me, in his own unique way. Hopefully, my scars will heal quicker this time, and I won't ache for him as much as I did in the past. As they say, first loves are the hardest to let go. And since Ryker has been my one and only love, it's a million times harder.

Delivering a parting kiss to his lips, Ryker pulls me off the floor and buttons his pants first before helping me into my panties and leggings. He picks up his wedding band off the tile and slips it back on his finger, cementing the end of our time together. Closure is what I needed, and perhaps he gave me just enough that I can move on and have a meaningful relationship in the future. Who knows what's in store.

Shoulders sagging, feet dragging, I grab the knob to open the door, but Ryker's hand stops me. Wrapping his arms around me from behind, his hands splaying over our daughter, he kisses the top of my head. For a few uninterrupted moments, we just breathe together, silently holding onto this time like neither of us want to step back into the real world. My insides twist at the thought, but I ignore it, just for a little while longer so I can bask in our daughter, who does a small tumble in my belly as if she knows he's here with us.

"I'm due March sixth," I whisper, not wanting to ruin the moment. "And yes, she's yours."

"You're giving me the three children I knew we'd always have. Thank you, Kat," he mutters into my hair, his voice ragged, clogged with emotion.

Folding my fingers through his atop my belly, we hold hands for sixteen heartbeats before I break our bond at the very second my sadness spills over, trailing two tears down my cheeks. I let them fall where they may. "You're welcome, Ryker," I murmur, and open the door, coming face to face with the reality that is my life, including a pregnant wife marching down the hallway, eyes on fire, ready to brawl.

"You fucking homewrecker!" she screeches, and Kade steps into her war path, blocking her way. Although I'm ready and more than willing to defend myself, if need be. Girls don't scare me a bit.

Ryker's hand on my back inches me forward, far enough that he can slip out of the bathroom to form an impenetrable wall in the middle of the hallway.

"Vanessa, we will not do this here," Ryker growls, crossing his arms over his impossibly large chest.

"You fucking slept with that whore, didn't you?!" I can't see her, but I can hear her fury as she huffs and stomps her foot like a three-year-old on the hardwood floor. Not that I blame her. I'd go crazy, too.

For half a second, I wait to feel guilty about what happened, but when I can't muster a single regret, I shrug it off and let Ryker handle his personal business. At least we settled some of our unfinished heartaches. That's one thing I thought I'd never be able to say.

Emotionally and physically drained, I lean against the wall next to the bathroom door and cross my ankles.

"That's none of your business," Kade interjects, instilling a sense of calmness into the atmosphere that lasts all of two beats before Vanessa's shrill voice slices it like a knife.

"It is, too! He's my husband!"

"He might be your old man. But she's the mother of his children, my friend, and you're not gonna start shit with her in our clubhouse or anywhere else. She's family. So it's time you learn some respect." Kade lays down the law, all stern and sexy as hell. It's quite the yummy sight to have two, big, brawny, dickalicious brothers guarding me when I don't really need their help. But, hey, what's a girl to do?

"I'm family, too!" Vanessa barks.

"No. You're—" Kade starts, but Ryker elbows his brother in the side.

"That's enough," he interjects.

"Hell no, it ain't." Kade elbows him back. "She's gotta learn her place."

"Why do you have to be such a dick, Kade? What did I ever do to you?" Vanessa asks.

"Don't," Ryker warns, except Kade isn't listening when he loses his shit.

"You're a child, Vanessa." His hand shoots forward. I can't see much, but I'm guessing that he's pointing at her. "A little girl who's been obsessed with my brother since you were eighteen. Don't think all of us haven't noticed. And don't you think for a fuckin' second you're some innocent bystander. You're not. You've been tryin' to bag him for years. But he's been too fucked in the head to give a damn about anyone. Then, what? You trap him when you mysteriously become pregnant after one drunken night, and he's too decent of a man to say fuck you, bitch, and walk away. Well, I'll tell you it to your face. Fuck you, you lying bitch. You come in here, acting all high and mighty 'cause you've got his property patch. A patch I know you begged for. Just like you begged him to marry your whore ass. If we're talkin' sluts here, Vanessa, you're the biggest of them all. How many of the brothers have you slept with? Most of 'em, aside from me, 'cause I know better. And my pops and Ghost 'cause their tastes don't lie in rank pussy."

A blood-curdling sob cuts through the air, making me feel a little sorry for the chick. But this isn't my fight. It's theirs. I've got enough on my plate. I just hope this ends soon because I'd like to go to bed.

"Yo-you're gonna let him talk to me like that?" she cries, addressing Ryker. From behind, I watch his shoulders lift and fall in a defeated shrug, his head dropping in shame. My fingers itch, wanting to reach out and touch him; to hold his hand and make it all better. Yeah. My conflicting emotions are crap. I know.

"We can talk about this at home, Vanessa," Ryker demands.

"You can't let your brother speak to me like that. That's not right. You picked me. We're having a baby!" she wails, reminding me so much of myself, years ago, when Ryker just up and vanished. At least she has him. She's right. He did pick her. They're having a baby. She should claim her prize before it's too late. Regardless of what Kade says, I don't see Ryker marrying a woman he doesn't love. There has to be something there, regardless if Kade likes her or not.

Being the bigger person, and so I can go to bed sooner rather than later, I push away from the wall, squeeze between two massive brothers who dwarf me considerably, and grab the side of Ryker's elbow, urging him forward. "Go talk to your wife. Work it out."

The words are like death and decay on my tongue, but it flows nonetheless. Refusing to make eye contact with anyone, I take a step back, retreating to the comfort of the wall, but the familiar arm of Kade reaches out and yanks me into his protective embrace. I bury my face in the side of his vest, inhaling the rich leather scent, struggling to ignore the spear that's lodged itself in my heart for doing the right thing. I bleed out, draining every ounce of hope away, and in its place, a hollowness resides.

I hate that I care this much. Even when I shouldn't.

"Listen to her, Ryker. I'm gonna take her to say goodnight to Pops and Ghost, then I'll put her in bed." Kade rubs my back in slow, reassuring strokes.

A hand that could be none other than Ryker's touches my shoulder for the briefest of moments. "Thank you for everything, Kat," he mutters one second, and he's gone the next, taking his angry wife with him.

Locked inside my mind with warring emotions, I function on autopilot. With an arm draped over my shoulder, Kade escorts me outside so I can say goodnight to my father. We hug, even though it barely registers. It's Bear's turn next, and he whispers some loving sentiment into my ear before Kade whisks me away, back to his bedroom, where he seems to understand what I'm going through without me having to explain. He doesn't pry.

Pushing my shoulders, I drop onto the bed and Kade undresses me. I let him, not caring if he sees me naked or not. It wouldn't be the first time. Once my clothes are discarded, he slips one of his oversized shirts over my head and tucks me into bed. Kissing my temple, he brushes my hair off my face and sets my glasses on the nightstand.

"I know it was a long day. If you wanna talk about anything, I'm here," he says, somewhere in the room.

There's a rustling of jeans and the *clank* of a belt hitting the floor. The bed dips next to me before it settles and a body inches from mine emits a soothing warmth. It's been ages since I've slept next to anyone. Scarlett and Roxie aren't allowed to sleep with me anymore because they're mini, comatose ninjas. I've gotten a bloody nose from Roxie once, as well as some ugly bruises. It's just not worth it anymore. No matter how lonely I get.

Flipping onto my side, facing him, I tuck my hand under my cheek as I curl my knees closer to get comfy. "You're sleepin' in bed with me?" I arch a tired brow, smirking.

"This is my bedroom, and I'm not gonna molest you if that's what you're worried about," he teases.

"You know I had sex with your brother, don't you?" I cut straight to the point.

He nods, his cheek smashed against the pillow, bare chest on open display, a sheet draped over his legs up to his navel. "Yes. I could hear you from the hall."

"You were out there the entire time?"

"Most of it, yeah. Ryker's been buggin' me all day to help him get a minute alone with ya."

"So you arranged it," I remark, then yawn, covering my mouth with my hand so he doesn't get a whiff of Thanksgiving breath.

"He did. I just followed his instructions."

"You were pretty mean to Vanessa," I comment because it's true.

Kade scoffs, rolling his eyes. "Right. I was mean. But she's been makin' googly eyes at Ryker for three years. It was only a matter of time she'd convince him to sleep with her. Then after one night, she's pregnant. I don't believe it."

"She's beautiful. Most men would give their left nut to screw her. And you *can* get pregnant that easily. Trust me."

The baby in my belly is case and point. One night of passion, and I've got another eighteen years looking at a little girl who will resemble her father through and through. Roxie and Scarlett are no different. They have his eyes, lips, and nose. The only things they've acquired from me are their blonde hair and paler skin. The rest is all Ryker. Especially Roxie's height. At nine, she's merely an inch shorter than me.

"I never wanted to fuck her. And, Ryker prefers blondes. Which I never understood until last night. Now it all makes sense."

"The broodiness and blondes, you mean?"

Kade licks his lips as if they're chapped. "Yep. So tell me about yourself, Kat."

"There's not much to tell." Nonchalantly, I shrug one shoulder.

"I'm sure there is. What do you do for fun?"

"Read books."

"Seriously?" His eyes round into saucers, and I have to bite my lip to keep from laughing in his face at his ridiculously, shocked expression.

"Yes." I chuckle quietly. "I read for fun. Watch a bit of TV. Cook some. And mostly take care of the girls. I don't get much me time. Not when I work full time, and have the girls' dance, school, and friend stuff to fit in. I'm only one person, so it's a lot to juggle. At night, after a long day, I drink a glass of wine and read a trashy romance novel to relax. Well..." I cup my belly. "Now I substitute my wine for juice, but I still drink it out of a wine glass, and pretend it's the same. Definitely not as exciting as your life, huh?" I wink.

"Not at all. But, my life doesn't usually have this much drama."

"Only when I pop in."

"Precisely." Kade baps me on the tip of my nose with his finger. "But I like it when you pop in."

"If I didn't know any better, Kade, I'd say you're flirtin' with me." Wiggling my eyebrows, I crack a silly grin.

Snickering, as a charming smile turns up at the corners of his full lips, he faintly shakes his head. "You're quite the woman."

My stomach dips at the praise, and I turn my face into the soft pillow to hide the evidence of my blush.

"I'm just me," I mumble into cotton, hoping he can hear.

The bed shakes, and I hear a tiny *click* sound before the room descends into darkness. "Goodnight, Kat. And Happy Thanksgiving. I'll see ya in the morning."

"Night, Kade." I flip onto my other side. Snuggling under the blankets, I tug them up to my shoulders. "Thank you for all your help."

"Anytime, pretty lady. Anytime."

PAST

The mouthwatering scent of bacon and pancakes drift through every room of the house, drawing my pregnant self out of the bedroom and into the kitchen.

"Mornin'," Brent sing-songs with a bouncy, blonde baby on his hip as he expertly flips another pancake onto a nearby plate.

Him cooking shouldn't look as sexy as it does, but those abs and that hip, V-thingy are extra delectable this morning thanks to those low-slung sweatpants. There's no way he's wearing any boxers either, because every time he moves, his dick swings, punching the fabric. I should have him cook like this for me more often. It's the best way to wake up. Especially after the shitty night I had. Eye candy and food—*score.*

Waddling over to the stool, I groan from exhaustion when my ass plops down at our small kitchen peninsula. Everything freaking aches—from my ham hock ankles to my sausage fingers, all the way up to my hair follicles. Giving birth to this baby can't come soon enough. I'm done. Ready to evict him or her out of this womb. You'd think with all of the uncomfortable sex we've had to coax the little terror out, that he'd get with the program. Guess not.

With a resounding *clank,* a stack of fluffy, golden pancakes, adorned with a bacon heart on top is set directly in front of me. Next to it, a smaller plate of additional bacon rests. Brent slides a bottle of syrup across the counter while Roxie babbles.

"Say good mornin' to your beautiful, tired mama, Rox," Brent says, hip resting against the cupboards, grinning at me like a lovesick puppy—even if he won't utter those words aloud.

Roxie makes some cute noises, and I reach across the counter to tickle her tiny baby toes that I wanna nibble all up. They're too damn cute. Don't you just love baby feet?

"Morning, Princess, and my sexy lover."

I force a bright smile. It's not so easy when all I want to do is sleep another twelve hours in hopes that this belly monster will crawl its way out of my tummy. I don't care what people tell you, being pregnant is only magical for the middle half of your pregnancy. In the beginning, you're miserable with

173

morning sickness. Unless you're one of those lucky unicorn bitches and don't get it. Then about three months in, you're hunky dory until the eight-month mark. Then it all goes to hell.

Yawning as I slather the pancakes in thick syrup, Brent asks, "Another bad night, huh?"

That's the understatement of the year.

Taking a bite of crispy bacon, I nod, chewing. "The worst," I mutter with my mouth still half full. Very ladylike, I know. "We've got ourselves a gold medalist swimming in here. Kept me up almost the entire night. I didn't even hear Rox this mornin'. Sorry about that." He shrugs one shoulder as if it wasn't a big deal, and I pat my beach ball sized bump. "Our swimmer finally decided to wear him or herself out at five. That's when I put my book down."

Wordlessly, Brent leans his upper body across the counter, and I know just what he's after, so I do my best to meet him halfway with a simple toe-curling, turn-me-on kiss. Okay. It's not simple at all. There's tongue, lots of it, and he tastes like bacon, which makes my stomach growl for more than food. Cupping the side of his face, his scruff abrading my palm in the hottest of ways, I lose myself in him, in us, in the most amazing man God could have ever created just for me.

A *thud* reverberates, dragging us from our haze. Blinking twice, my brain whirls as I watch our daughter slap her entire palm in a puddle of spilled syrup on the countertop. Brent and my eyes collide for the briefest of seconds before we lose it—cackling like two silly hyenas. Roxie giggles right along with us as Daddy sets her on the counter to play in her sugary mess, and tosses the half-empty bottle in the sink.

Stickiness coating her kick-happy legs, feet, and fingers, Roxie lifts a dripping fist to her mouth to taste. A squeal of delight booms in our quaint kitchen as she suckles the mapley goodness. Her infectious happiness hits me square in the chest, forcing me to laugh right alongside her, smiling until my cheeks hurt.

Leaning over the peninsula again, Brent pecks my lips, beaming. "You look quite yummy," he murmurs to my mouth, and Rox slaps his cheek with a hand coated in syrup and baby drool. Chuckling, he quickly turns his head and sucks our daughter's fingers into his mouth. Roxie tries to pry them away, giggling hysterically, but he won't let go.

"Ummm ... I think I should eat Roxie's hand all up. It tastes sooooo gooood. Nom, nom, nom," he teases, making loud munching sounds as he pretends to devour her wiggling fingers. She loves every second of it. Excited tears stream down her cheeks, her face beet red from laughing so hard that she can barely catch her breath. I find myself with my own happy tears forming as Daddy steals her other hand to gobble it clean like the cookie monster.

Trapped in the moment, I nearly miss the tightness that envelopes my belly at the exact second a gush of water expels from my lady parts, soaking my pajama pants and legs before pooling on the hardwood floor beneath the stool.

Eyes shooting wide, gasping in shock, I cup my hardening stomach. "Oh, crap! I think it's time to have our baby!"

PRESENT

"What'll ya have, sweetie?" a middle-aged waitress with red bouffant hair, and *Walmart* blue eye shadow asks while snapping her bubble gum. I swore these kinds of women only existed in movies. Yet, here I am, seated in a red vinyl booth, inside a greasy spoon diner, looking up at this lady, who's waiting for me to pick something to eat off their oversized plastic menu.

"Pancakes and bacon." I nod once, confirming my order to myself, before handing back the menu, which she tucks under her arm before turning to Kade for his order.

"Same. And some coffee, too, please. Black," he replies before she gets a chance to ask.

"Sure, sweetie. Comin' right up." The woman slides Kade's unused menu off the table and strides away.

"Pancakes, huh?" he inquires with both arms stretched coolly over the back of the booth, making him look like some 1950's badass biker. Sorta like the

Fonz, but not. "Thought you'd be more like an oatmeal with dried fruit kinda chick."

Mock offended, I clutch at my chest. "Oh. You wound me, sir. If you must know, I used to love pancakes, but I haven't had any in ... about eight years." That's the most I'm going to divulge on the subject, so I hope he doesn't press for more. Usually, I'm more of a bagel and cream cheese person, or the occasional bowl of cereal—the kind that has too much sugar but tastes too darn good to pass up. Scarlett and Roxie are cuckoo for *Cocoa Puffs* every time we hit the grocery.

Honestly, I haven't eaten pancakes since that morning all of those years ago when Scarlett came barreling out of my vagina less than thirty minutes after my water broke in our kitchen. Brent vanished a few months later. I think maybe he took my taste for mapley breakfast with him. Except this morning, of all days. Perhaps it's because I've gotten a slight bit of closure. I don't know, and don't really care. That fluffy, syrupy yumminess is sounding awfully appealing right about now, so I'm going to gorge myself until I pop. Today seems as good of a day as ever, since I'm leaving in a matter of hours to drive to the airport.

This morning, Kade woke me up at the butt crack of dawn. Okay. It was more like eight, but it felt too damn early. Then he'd goaded me out of bed with the promise of a fun excursion before my flight. It worked. I took a quick shower, dressed in these jeggings, and a flouncy, white, maternity shirt. My feet and ankles have finally stopped swelling, so I was

177

able to fit into my flats again. We then snuck out of the house, and into his oversized *Dodge* pickup before anyone knew we'd escaped. It felt a little like breaking out of jail, and I cherished every heart-pounding second of it.

Driving into the nearby town, he'd given me the unofficial tour. Which, I have to admit, wasn't much. This is the closest town of any importance within a forty mile radius, and it's quite tiny. We'd driven past the hospital that looked more like a small veterinarian's office. There are no chain restaurants or stores anywhere; not even a *McDonalds* or *Subway*. One could swear that they're around every darn corner. Just not in Red Fort, Texas. They do have four small restaurants, one of which is *Red's Diner*, where we're seated right now. The other three are mom and pop places—a pizza joint, dairy bar-deli combo, and a steakhouse of some sort. It looked like the most promising of the establishments with its grand windows, frilly awnings, and brick walls. They don't serve breakfast, so that's why we're here.

Our waitress delivers my water with a lemon wedge dropped inside, and Kade's coffee in an ever cliché white mug. I take a tentative sip from my straw and cross my ankles under the table. "So, why'd ya bring me here?" We haven't spoken much, aside from his basic guidemanship that consisted of pointing to a building or landmark and explaining what it was. Hell, I'm pretty sure that's not a word, but he was my guide for all intents and purposes, so guidemanship it is.

Kade timidly shrugs both shoulders. "Figured you could use the distraction. And I thought you'd like to see how your dad has lived since he..." leaning forward until his stomach touches the edge of the table, Kade cups his hand on the side of his mouth like he's about to tell me a secret, "*died*," he whispers, bouncing his eyebrows.

Ah....

I smirk.

"Um ... okay then. What else is left to show me? There's not much here."

Which is true. They do have a post office, and a trailer-sized sheriff's department, that Kade said houses two inmates at a time. There is no courthouse or fancy clothing stores. They have an Outpost, which has the essential apparel, ammunition, and stuff. Or that's what the front window said when we drove past. I did see a grocery store. One that was larger than I expected, compared to the size of the town. It even had carts outside. That was impressive in itself. We'd passed a single pump gas station/bait shop. It had a large tin sign on its weather-worn siding that read *'worms here'*. And I'd gotten a good look at the hotel I'd booked, yet never stayed at. It wasn't much more than a house with a sign out front. More like a rundown bed and breakfast. All in all, it's a charming little village. Not much to look at, but it does have its appeal, nonetheless. A simple way of living, I suppose. It even has a single school that doesn't look much bigger than our high school back at home. Although, it did appear more modern than I expected, with its nice playground equipment and all.

Not sure why I noticed that, but I did. That'll be perfect for when Ryker and Vanessa's child starts school there. Time flies faster than ya know it. All they have to do is blink, and their kid will be born, out of diapers, and going to school for the first time. It seems like only yesterday Scarlett was welcomed into this world. Now she's in third grade.

"Nope, it's a pretty boring place. Only got one bar, and it doesn't even have women takin' their tops off." He sips his coffee, and I shake my head, fighting a smile and losing miserably.

"Is that all you think about is naked women?"

"I'm a man. I may respect chicks, but I think about tits fifty percent of the day."

"And what do you think about the other fifty?"

Kade grins, taking an extra-long drink from his mug, eyes mischievously dancing over the rim. "The other fifty I'm thinkin' about their mouths on my dick, or my dick in their pussies. Sometimes both at the same time."

On impulse, my hand shoots across the space between us and I slap his bicep. "You're a pig." I bark a laugh, and our waitress interrupts at the perfect time, setting our mountainous stacks of pancakes and plates of bacon in front of us. Without pause, I pour syrup over the golden discs and dive right on in. The first bite is like an orgasm exploding on my tongue. I moan, chewing, and Kade gruffly clears his throat.

I forgot how *good* these tasted.

"Can you not do that?" he mumbles, tearing into a piece of bacon.

I swallow and gulp some water before replying. "Do what?"

"Stop making noises when you eat."

Forking another piece of flapjack, it's halfway to my lips when I frown at him, brows furrowing. "What do you mean? I like my food. It's good." I shovel it into my mouth, groaning erotically to spite him.

"You're moaning, and it's distracting the customers," he whisper screams as if people are staring. They're not. Okay, maybe that guy in the corner who just put down his newspaper glanced over. Everyone else is too preoccupied to notice my food pleasure, and if I had to guess, somebody is sexually frustrated.

I cut another piece with the edge of my fork. "Are you horny, Kade? 'Cause it looked like you got plenty of action last night. So you should be fine."

Rubbing his forehead with three fingers, and expelling a sigh, he shakes his head twice. "Woman, you can't be talkin' like that."

"Talkin' like what? Your dick gettin' sucked? Pretty sure I got a free, softcore porn show of it last night. If it hadn't been for your woman's deep throatin' talents, I'd have gotten the full view of your johnson," I comment, like we're talking about the weather. Part of me knows I should be mortified by this conversation, while the part I'm actually taking comfort in, knows I'm damn justified.

The man in the booth behind me chokes on something. Apparently, he's been eavesdropping on our conversation. I look over my shoulder to address him. "Sir, is my food moaning a distraction? Or is it the porn discussion?"

He chokes again before clearing his throat. And I pay no attention to Kade's obvious growl of irritation.

Peering over his shoulder, the man grins shyly, his cheeks fire engine red. "Ma'am, I'm sorry. I see plenty of the club members in here, but I don't think I've seen them bring many women. And certainly not one as candid as you."

"Just ignore her, Frank. I am," Kade grumbles.

Turning sideways in my seat, I rest my knee on the booth, and my elbow on the back to get more comfortable. "Frank, is it? I'm Katrina. It's a pleasure to meet you." I offer the handsome fifty-something man my hand, and we shake. It's awkward from this position.

"Likewise, Katrina. You new to Red Fort, or just passin' through?"

"Just came for Thanksgiving. Headed home today," I answer out of courtesy.

"Hope you have safe travels then." He politely dips his chin toward me then swings his gaze to Kade. "See ya around, bud. Don't be givin' this one any more porn shows than necessary." There's a twinkle in his brown eyes as he smiles at us, throws some cash on his table, and exits the booth.

Turning around, I tuck back into my glorious meal, trying my best not to moan anymore, even if these pancakes are fantastic. A comfortable silence hangs in the air between us as we devour our food with little decorum. It's nice that I don't have to worry about what he'll think if I gorge myself. I'm pregnant, so I get a pass. Something tells me Kade wouldn't care what I ate, even if I wasn't as big as a van. I like that about him. After dating a health freak who gave me the stink eye every time I chose beef over chicken, I decided no more judgy eaters in my life. It's not worth the added stress.

Kade finishes first, and the waitress swiftly carts away the dirty dishes after topping off his coffee. He pulls his phone from his pocket and checks something on the screen. "You've got an hour before we gotta leave for the airport."

"We?" I ask around a bite of bacon.

"Pops and I are gonna follow you in my truck."

"Why aren't you riding your motorcycles? Don't bikers usually ride, ya know, bikes?"

He puts his phone away. "Yeah, but if we don't wanna stick out like sore thumbs, we gotta use the truck. Discretion is key."

"'Cause you don't want bad guys coming after me if they find out I've been down here, and that my dad is still breathin'."

"Who the fuck told you that?" Kade barks. Sitting up straighter, eyes on high alert, he scans the place as if we're seated in the middle of a war zone. Someone needs to take a chill pill.

Silently observing his jerky movements, I sip my water, not the least bit concerned. "Your brother," I reply.

"What else did he tell you?"

Great, now he's mad. I probably should've kept my trap shut about anything Ryker said. They're most likely some MC secrets that he's gonna get in trouble for telling me. Sheesh, now I'm feeling guilty as hell. What if he does get in trouble because of my big mouth?

"Nothing," I fib, polishing off the last morsel of maple saturated pancake. Cleaning my sticky lips with the sweep of my tongue, I stare at my plate. Would it be bad if I licked it spotless? Or is that going too far? I wonder if Kade would even notice.

"Do you want more pancakes, beautiful?" He half-chuckles, easing back into the booth, shoulders relaxing.

Demurely, I dabble the corners of my mouth with a napkin. "Was I drooling?"

"No, but you looked like someone just kicked a puppy. You like pancakes that much, do ya?"

Noncommittally, I shrug one shoulder. "I used to."

"So are you gonna tell me what else Ryker told ya about these bad men?"

"Not if it's gonna get him into trouble."

Kade nods in some sort of macho man approval, humming. "Good girl. That's the right answer. You don't gotta tell me anything. But I will say whatever my brother said is true. He's just lookin' out for your best interest, even if he's a dick about everything else."

Right. Okay. I didn't come here to talk about Ryker. I've barely thought about him all morning. Well ... that's a massive lie. I've thought about him since I woke up. The residual burn of last night's kiss still lingers on my lips, and my girl bits are tingly. All because of him, and his too-sexy self. I promise it's not deliberate. I'm not *trying* to think about it. But he's just there lingering in the back of my mind, making me wonder things like... Is Vanessa still pissed at him? Did he confess to us having sex? Does he hate me? Is he okay? Does he feel he got some closure, too?

Stuck in my head, over thinking too much, I don't notice Kade slipping out of the booth until he's standing, waiting patiently for me to surf through my jumbled thoughts. When I finally glance up at his towering form, he offers me his hand. "Come on, beautiful. I've got some houses to show you."

Driving through Red Fort's only trailer park, Kade thumb points to an off-yellow, single-wide with gnarly weeds eating it alive. Apparently, this park doesn't have rules about lawn maintenance because that looks downright awful. "That's Bongo's trailer."

"Who the hell is Bongo?" I didn't meet him last night, or any of the other people whose houses he drove me past. Pretty sure I'd remember their names.

"He's one of our *special* members... As you can see, there's not much down here to make people wanna join a club. But we've got the highest member rate out of all our chapters. Twenty-nine and counting."

I incline my head toward the beaten up tin box. "And why do people like this Bongo live down here? Couldn't they join elsewhere?"

"See, that's the thing. Our club's for the misfits who didn't get along with members of their chapter. Or it's for those the club wants to keep under tight lock and key."

"What the heck does that mean?"

"That means, members like Bongo serve a purpose for the club. A purpose they don't want a lot of people knowin' about. And down here, there's nobody to worry about causin' trouble for us. The townsfolk like keepin' us around, 'cause we keep the riffraff out."

"So these members are like, what? Mercenaries?" I ask, absentmindedly rubbing my daughter. She's been fairly active since I fed her all that sugar.

"Some of 'em are." Keeping his explanations oddly vague, he drives on, taking a left out of the trailer park. Up ahead, in the middle of a small forest, is a small blue house with white shutters. Flicking his chin in its direction, he slows the truck to a crawl. "That's Roscoe and Hammer's place. They decided to shack up. Didn't wanna fit the extra housing bill. Not that the cost of livin' is much."

I sideways glance at Kade, who looks right at home behind the wheel. Peaceful even. Surprisingly, I haven't seen his knife all day. I'm going to go out on a limb and say that's a good thing. "What do they do for the club? Or am I not allowed to ask that?" I pry.

"They're just the muscle. Nothin' fancy. They patched over around the same time from other chapters. Pops has done a fine job keepin' 'em in line.

186

They were cocky little fucks when we took 'em in. Your dad might not be able to do a whole lot on the outside for the club, Kat, but he sure as hell knows how to keep fuckers in line. Pop straightens 'em out, then your dad keeps 'em that way. He dictates their every move. Tells 'em where to go and what they're doing. That's what makes him such an asset to us. Granted, I'm not supposed to tell ya any of this. Though, considerin' you're family, what's it gonna hurt if I tell ya just a bit?"

"I'm not going to say anything." And I won't. I'll take their secrets to the grave with me.

Kade pulls away, the twang of country music barely audible in the cab as we ride on. Watching building after building pass by in a monotonous blur, we come to the outskirts of town where houses are few and far between. Eventually, he veers to the side of a country road and parks along the grassy shoulder in front of a rustic cabin. It is set in the middle of a wooded area that's off the road a ways back. If it weren't for the small gravel drive and a few fallen trees, you wouldn't be able to make out the place. The dark stained, log exterior blends into the scenery quite well—it's absolutely stunning, the craftsmanship second to none. From the charming porch swing, spindly posts, and the two-toned shutters, it looks like an adult version of a gingerbread house. If gingerbread houses were rustic log cabins.

The ignition is turned off, and Kade nods toward the building. "That's Ryker's place. He bought the land shortly after he came home. Then he built that cabin all by himself. Wouldn't let anybody help him. He lives there alone, sometimes, while Vanessa stays in the trailer he bought her. It's in that park we just drove through. Nobody's been in the cabin but him. And he doesn't stay there much. Most of the time, he's at the clubhouse in our spare room, or at Vanessa's. Wasn't sure why he kept the house if he's never gonna live there."

A crushing tightness in my chest makes it hard for me to breath, let alone talk. Why would he show me this? Why does it matter?

"Why'd you bring me here?" I choke out, my voice betraying every emotion that's battling in my head and ... heart.

I can't explain why, but my vision hazes as it fills with unshed tears. Carefully, as to not draw attention to myself, I remove my glasses and set them in my lap before swiping the wetness away. I've done enough crying in my life. Looking at that sad and lonely little cabin shouldn't make me so ... whatever this is. It's just a wooden box with walls and a porch. Nothing more. Though, it feels like so much more. Like I'm getting a secret piece of Brent back. Not to keep. But to understand and cherish for just a little while.

Eyes fixed on the forest, Kade's hand slides across the top of the seat and comes to rest on my knee. He pats me there, strong and supportive—just like the man himself. "As angry as I may be with my family right now, I realize this has gotta be just as hard for everyone else. Especially my brother. He's been livin' in this hell for years, knowin' he's got two daughters out there that he couldn't tell anyone about. I never understood him bein' a prick before. Or why he built this cabin if he had no intention of livin' in it. Or why he and Ghost stopped gettin' along when he came home. Now it's all startin' to make sense. That's why I wanted to bring ya into town. Not only to show ya a bit of your dad's life—which, as you can see by Red Fort, isn't much. I also wanted ya to see this. Because I think he'd want you to know about it, even if he can't tell you himself."

Wiping more tears away, that won't stop forming, I lay my palm over Kade's. It's warm, and I focus on that instead of everything else I need to try and forget. I didn't come to Texas to deal with my Brent issues. I came for my dad. And here I am, at peace with my father. Whereas, my internal battle with Ryker has merely begun.

"Thank you," I mutter, slipping my glasses back on.

Kade squeezes my knee. "Anytime, beautiful. I know it's shitty with Ryker bein' married, and all the shit you've got goin' on. But I know ya still care about him, and he, you. Do you wanna get out and look at it?"

My heart flips over in my chest as a shiver passes through me. Yes, I want to explore the entire property, but I'm not going to. "Wouldn't that be trespassing?"

"What Ryker don't know, can't hurt him."

"Yes. But I'd know. And if he wanted people to see it, he'd let them. I don't wanna take away his privacy."

"You're too damn good of a woman. I hope you know that."

"I don't, but thank you."

For a few unspoiled beats, we sit in peace, watching the tree branches sway in front of the empty cabin. Then, as if he knows when I'm ready, Kade turns the ignition and pulls away. It's a heart aching moment, yet the perfect ending to an otherwise irreplaceable couple of days. I'm sad to leave. Though, it'll be nice to see my girls again. I miss them like crazy, and I'm sure they're driving grandma nuts. I haven't spoken to them since yesterday. When I get to the airport, I'll be sure to shoot Mom a quick text.

Turning up the music, Kade's hand still on my leg, we listen to country songs all the way back to the clubhouse. Dad is waiting for us on the front porch when we arrive. Next to his feet is my duffle bag. Bear is right behind him, shutting the front door in his wake, a sad smile playing on his ruggedly handsome face as he turns and lifts a chin in our direction. He sets a hand on Dad's shoulder as the truck comes to a stop a few feet from the steps and I climb out.

"It's time to go, Peanut. Kade said he'd taken ya to breakfast. What'd ya think of Red Fort?" Dad's arms stretch wide as I walk up the steps and fold myself into his embrace, my own arms curling around his back in a big hug.

Nose stuffed against his chest, the scent of leather and him swirling in my brain intensifies our bittersweet farewell. I'm going to miss this most. "It was small. But nice."

He squeezes me tight until I fear I might pop. "There's not much to see, but I'm glad ya got to visit before ya left."

"Me, too," I wheeze, unable to inhale fully.

"Ghost, I think you're holdin' her too tight. Let her go and give her the phone." Bear steers us away from the brink of an emotional breakdown. Okay, my breakdown. The tears are welling again. Damn female hormones. Blinking them away, I reluctantly pry myself from Dad's arms.

Kade honks the horn, his head hanging out of the driver side window. "I know it sucks to say goodbye, but we gotta go unless you want her to be late!" he hollers.

"Hold the fuck up, son!" Bear growls.

"You've got one minute!" Kade returns and my sadness sinks to an all-time low.

Hooking a finger under my chin, Dad tips my face up and places a gentle kiss on my cheek. "I love you. We're gonna keep in touch. I promise. Bear and I have already talked it out." Releasing me, he produces a small black phone from his jeans pocket. "This is yours. It's got Kade's, mine, and Bear's numbers programmed in. You can't contact us from your cell. It's not safe. But this one's secure. You can call or text us anytime you want, day or night."

My bottom lip wobbles and I take the phone, clutching it in my hand like a lifeline. "Okay. Thanks. I love you, too."

Bear kisses Dad on the temple as he scoots around us, grabs my bag, and crunches his heavy boots across the gravel, tossing my stuff into the back of

Kade's pickup. Without a word, he climbs into the cab with his son, giving me the father-daughter sendoff I've needed since the day he died.

Taking Dad's hands into mine, phone smashed in between, I hold onto him for dear life, staring into his eyes that look just like mine. "I'm glad I came." I sound horrible. My voice is all scratchy on the verge of a total meltdown. Swallowing hard, I try to dislodge the knot in my throat. It refuses to budge.

"Me, too. Now be careful, and text me as soon as you land. And then when you get home."

Grinning at his overprotectiveness, I bow my head in compliance. "I will…"

Before I lose the nerve and start bawling my damned eyes out, I hug my dad one last time and sprint over to my rental car. Well, I try to run. It's more like a fast waddle, and probably looks hilarious, but I make it there and lock myself inside. The keys are in the ignition and my phone in the cup holder. These men think of everything. I set my new phone next to my old and turn the car on.

Kade expertly backs his truck out of the lane first. Then I follow suit, slowly, trying to stay on the gravel. Reaching the road, I stop just at the entrance of driveway and wave to my dad, who's standing on the porch, his eyes swollen and red. He swipes them once with the back of his hand and returns my wave. Quickly, I blow him a kiss, then take off, tires screeching as I shoot past Kade and Bear in the truck. They let me drive like a crazy lady without honking or calling to give me shit. I need this, the distraction, so I don't turn around, throw myself back into my dad's arms, and beg him to come home with me. Which isn't where he belongs. Not anymore. This is his home now, with Bear, the man he loves, and the club that's accepted him. A place that a woman like me doesn't belong.

Flipping a radio station on, music blaring as loud as it can go, I cry. The torrent of jumbled emotions pour, using my face as their outlet. And I let them. I weep from happiness, sadness, pain, heartache, and, most of all, I cry for the lost years of what could have been.

The drive goes quicker than I expect, and soon, I'm pulling into the rental car lot, returning my vehicle. The man at the counter is kind enough that he doesn't stare at my blotchy face when I drop off the keys. Kade and Bear are parked outside the building when I return to the lovely warmth of the outdoors, which'll soon turn to bitter cold when I get home to Indiana. *Blah.* That's one thing I don't miss there. Sure, the four seasons are beautiful, but staying warm year round is better.

Stepping out of the passenger side, Bear helps me into the front seat before slipping into the back of the crew cab. We don't speak as a dense cloud of gloom cloaks the cab the closer we get to the terminal gates.

Parking in the unloading area, Kade grabs my hand, stopping me from going anywhere, at the same moment I push my door open. Folding our fingers together, a calmness settles over me, scaring away my heavy heart and filling it with a flicker of hope. I might be leaving, but that doesn't mean forever. It's hard to remember that when you're faced with the ugly truth that you're flying home by yourself and leaving a whole new family behind.

"It's not gonna be forever, Kat. We're only a flight or phone call away," Kade explains, his words rushed and gruffer than usual like he's trying to convince himself more than me. It's good to know I'm not the only one dreading my departure. That makes me feel loved.

Afraid to talk, I dip my head in a solitary nod. Realistically, I know what he says is true. That doesn't make any of this easier. Not since I haven't heard a thing from Ryker. And my dad couldn't see me off ... because of him bein' dead and all.

Schooling my features, I unfold my fingers from Kade's and carefully climb out of the truck. Bear and Kade follow, dragging their feet almost as badly as me.

Standing outside the sliding doors of the airport, Bear grudgingly offers me the handles of my duffle, and I accept them, but not without a small game of tug of war. "I should really carry this inside for you, darlin'." He tries to steal it back, but I'm not having that.

I hug the bag to my chest.

"Bear, it's fine. You didn't have to follow me here in the first place," I reason.

Kade claps his dad on the shoulder. "Let's get this over with before we start cryin' like little bitches, and needin' tampons and *Midol*."

All three of us chuckle at his attempt to lighten the mood. It works for a second. Our hugs are quick and painless. Bear's is fiercer than Kade's. They wish me a safe flight before I waddle my way inside to check my bag and claim my boarding pass.

Caught up in my own thoughts, everything passes in a blur. From the security check and droning announcements, all the way to the uncomfortable chairs I have to sit in to wait for my row to be called. It's all so impersonal and lonely.

Clutching my carry-on to my chest, I hoist my behind out of the chair the minute my boarding order is announced over the loudspeaker. Men, women, and children stand in a single file line, waiting to be scanned in so they can load into the airplane. Sometimes I find myself wondering what their stories are. Where they come from. Why they're flying in the same box in the sky as me. It keeps me occupied a little while longer, as I smile politely to the flight attendant who *beeps* me in, and I make my final trek to my seat.

Knowing that I'll have to use the restroom more than once, I opted for an aisle seat a couple rows from the bathrooms. They're not the easiest to maneuver around in when you're the size of a house, but it's better than peeing yourself. A business man with graying hair and kind eyes takes the middle seat, while a teenager with bright pink headphones claims the window. Buckling in, I take a deep breath and decide right here, and now I will not cry anymore. This is not a sad goodbye. It was one trip that gave me closure and the happy possibility for more. What kind of more, I don't know for sure.

Setting my purse into my lap, I unzip the top to shut down my phones since I know they can't be on—

aerospace rules. When I reach inside, my hand bumps into the corner of something sharp—a folded letter, just like those you got back in school, and a black box.

Baffled, my trembling fingers unfold the paper, and my breath catches.

To my little Tiger,

Last night was the most amazing night I've had in years. It doesn't top our first Thanksgiving, but I'd call it a close second. You're more beautiful than I remembered. So full of life that it hurt to watch. Not in a bad way. Just ... fuck ... I don't know. You're remarkable. How's that for shitty explanations?

There is so much I've wanted to say, but couldn't find the words to express how truly sorry I am. I know I've broken your heart more than once, and I'll never be able to forgive myself for that.

I can't pour my heart out onto a piece of paper. That's never worked out well for me. So I'm going to leave you with a gift instead. Please open the box now.

Complying with the letter, I do as I'm told and lift the lid off, setting it onto my thigh. Inside are three blue organza bags with necklaces coiled in each.

Returning to the letter, I read on.

I noticed you weren't wearing the infinity necklace I bought you years ago. I'm not sure if it broke or you threw it out because of the bastard I am. But please accept these, for you and our daughters. I know it's not much. And you can tell them they're from you. I don't care. Just knowing they have them is what matters.

I truly am sorry for everything.
Be happy.
Forever, Your Asshole.

Sucking back emotions through my shimmery gaze, I inspect each delicate necklace. One is silver with a rhinestone R charm dangling in the center. The other is the same with an S instead—our daughters' initials. But when I come to mine, the letter A is staring back at me.

Why in the hell would he give me a letter A?

Removing it from the bag and running my nail over the bridge of the A, something clicks into place, and I can't help it when I laugh out loud. Full belly, rumbling giggles have me doubling over, as people gawk, wondering if I've lost my mind. But I don't care. I laugh, and I laugh until there's not a breath left in my lungs and my eyes are matted with tears that aren't from sadness.

Asshole.

He gave me a fucking Asshole necklace.

That silly man truly knows my heart better than I do to give me a necklace that I will surely wear just to display my love/hate for him. He's a genius. Although I would never tell him that. Not that I'll ever speak to him again.

Slipping the note and all of the gifts except mine into the purse, I fasten the damned thing around my neck to wear with pride. Smiling the entire flight home, I think about the asshole who may have ruined me, but gave me a smidge of closure just the same.

The End...
For Now...

Playlist

1. James Bay- 'Let It Go'

2. James Bay- 'Incomplete'

3. James Bay- 'Hold Back The River'

4. Staind- 'It's Been A While'

5. Daughtry- 'Crawling Back To You'

6. Jennifer Nettles- 'Unlove You'